THE SLA
OF SHADOWS

Elana Bregin

THE BODLEY HEAD
LONDON

For my family with deep love.
And for Lliane, whose encouragement helped me to persevere.

1 3 5 7 9 10 8 6 4 2
Copyright © Elana Bregin 1995

Elana Bregin has asserted her right under the Copyright, Designs and
Patents Act, 1988 to be identified as the author of this work

First published in the United Kingdom 1995
by The Bodley Head Children's Books
Random House, 20 Vauxhall Bridge Road, London SW1V 2SA

Random House Australia (Pty) Limited
20 Alfred Street, Milsons Point, Sydney,
New South Wales 2061, Australia

Random House New Zealand Limited
18 Poland Road, Glenfield,
Auckland 10, New Zealand

Random House South Africa (Pty) Limited
PO Box 337, Bergvlei 2012, South Africa

Random House UK Limited Reg. No. 954009

A CIP record for this book is available from the British Library

ISBN 0 370 32410 2

Typeset by SX Composing Ltd, Rayleigh, Essex
Printed and bound in Great Britain by Mackays of Chatham Plc,
Chatham, Kent

One

I was eight years old the first time that I saw him, the Slayer of Shadows. I remember the moment very well. It was a very hot day and the Jungle was sizzling in its ugliness with all its excrement smells. I was sitting in the alleyway between the Jondolos,* letting the sun melt me, watching the silver sweat drip off the corrugations of the shacks. When suddenly I felt a coolness flowing over me. And when I looked up, there he was. He smiled at me and said something. But I didn't hear what it was. I only heard the colours in his voice. The sun made a rainbow around him. I couldn't look away from his brightness. He was dressed in green, like a garden. His skin was deep brown, as mine was. But his hair was the yellow of the sun. He seemed like a god to me, like the sun-god himself, stepped down from the sky into our Jungle. And I knew right away that he was sent to save me. I could tell from the start that he was a Slayer of Shadows.

He spoke to me again. He said, 'What are you

* shacks

1

doing here in the heat, little sister? This sun will melt your bones into puddles if you're not careful.'

'I am listening to the cockroaches,' I told him. Even then you see, even at that young age, I had the gift – the curse. Except that then, I didn't know it. I thought that everyone saw and heard the way I did. As though the world's skin was transparent, and you could see right through to the insides of things.

The Shadow-slayer smiled at my answer, and crouched down in order to look me in the eyes. His own eyes were yellow, like his hair, full of power; yet with a kindness in them.

'And what are they saying, these cockroaches?' he asked me.

'They are speaking of their hunger,' I told him. 'They are complaining that there is nothing to eat here any more.'

His smile disappeared. I saw his eyes examining my thinness. 'Are they very hungry then, these poor cockroaches?'

I nodded my head. 'There is no food anywhere. Not even in the rubbish piles. The rats have taken it all.'

My words kept him silent for a moment.

'I wish I could help them,' he said sadly. 'It is terrible for anything to be so hungry. Even cockroaches.'

He patted his pockets, and I heard their emptiness sigh.

'I have nothing to give the cockroaches,' he said. 'But I have something for you, little sister.' He took off his watch and put it into my hand, closing my fingers around it.

'This isn't worth much money. But maybe you can find a trader who will exchange it for some food,' he said. 'A bag of rice or mielie* meal at least. Don't give it away for less.'

He asked me then what my name was. I told him I didn't have one. I did of course. But I didn't like it much. It was a word that meant Sorrow – because the day I was born was the day our house was burned down in the fighting; that was the first time. My mother named me out of her despair. I always felt the name was like a curse.

My answer made the Shadow-slayer smile again.

'Everyone must have a name,' he said. 'Well then, I'll have to give you one. I'll call you . . . Marinda! That means – the pretty girl who talks with cockroaches.'

I liked that name very much. I liked the way he said it, with the sound of a song inside it. I asked him what his name was. He told me it was Zach.

'Zach!' I said. And the word was like a yellow fire, lighting up my mind. I knew what that name meant, though I didn't say it. It meant the Shadow-slayer. It meant the Bringer of Hope.

'Well, goodbye pretty Marinda. Perhaps I'll see you here again another day,' Zach said. He touched my cheek briefly, then walked on down the alley.

Where he'd been standing, flowers had sprung up. And the air was full of bright butterflies. I watched the halo of his hair disappear into the twisting maze of shacks beyond the alley. I heard

* maize meal

3

the whispering of the cockroaches, urgent and sharp. I got up and hurried after him.

The green trail of his passage was easy to follow through the Jungle's arid colours. Shadows twitched, sullen and listless as I ran past them. The baked ground burned my feet. Yet I scarcely felt it. On the next corner, a pack of scavengers stood lounging idly, their ferret eyes swivelling to watch Zach striding by. I held my breath, waiting for them to fall on him and rip him to pieces, as they sometimes do with strangers. But they let him pass unharmed. They read the sign of his hair and they were afraid to touch him, lest some wizardry befall them. The unusual is often a sign of witch-craft in our Jungle. Sorcerers mark themselves with various deformities in order that their power shall be known; odd-coloured eyes, shoulder humps, six-fingered hands, carbuncled noses. Even jakkals give such persons a wide berth, fear-ing the torments that their black spells might unleash.

I caught up with the Shadow-slayer beside the smouldering ruins of a shack that had burnt in the night. I could hear rats feeding inside, and the pro-test of tortured corpse flesh. Zach turned in surprise to find me beside him.

'Marinda! What are you doing here, little sister? You mustn't follow me,' he said. 'It's not safe for one so small as you to go wandering alone through this snakes' pit. Children vanish here. Come, show me where you live and I'll take you home.'

'I don't want to go home,' I said. 'I want to go with you.'

He laughed a little, ruffling my thin fuzz of hair.

'Where I am going is too far for little legs,' he said.

'And once we get there, who would bring you home again, do you think? You'd have to walk all the way back by yourself.'

'I wouldn't come back,' I said. 'I'd stay there, with you.'

He laughed again, very gently, the sun caught in his yellow eyes.

'What would your poor parents say to that?' he chided. 'Think how they'd worry if you just disappeared that way, and they didn't know where you were.'

'I haven't got parents,' I told him. 'The jakkals burnt them. They burn everything,' I said. 'There is only my grandmother left now. But she's old and sick and has no money to keep me. She won't mind if you take me to live with you.'

Zach looked at me for a long time without saying anything.

'I'd like to meet your grandmother. Will you take me to her?' he asked. He took my hand. And we walked back together through the Jungle shadows. I felt the jakkals drooling as they looked at me. I felt the sharp thoughts of the vultures, rearing for my eyes. But the Shadow-slayer's brightness made a charmed web around me, his confidence was like a sword that cleaved a way through for us both.

Two

Our Jondolo, where my grandmother and I lived, was a very ugly place. It was damp and dark and falling to pieces. But the worst thing about it was the smell. It was infested with shadows. The stench of dead bodies and blood was very bad in there. Sometimes, it was hard to walk inside at all. The family who had lived there before us had been murdered – all ten of them, including the toddler of two – shot to pieces by some war party seeking revenge for a death in their own ranks. It was often that way in our Jungle. Innocents died – convenient scapegoats for the blood-lust of others, while the real culprits went free. Then those deaths would, in turn, require avenging. And there would be more slaughter, more innocents to avenge.

Some nights, you couldn't sleep for the howls of the dead dishonoured, goading the living on to acts of retribution in their name. Often, in our Jondolo, I'd wake to see the corpses of the slaughtered family of ten, groaning and gnashing their teeth on the floor beside me – even the youngest.

And I'd watch their ghosts get up and walk out through the walls in search of vengeance. I'd lie there, waiting and trembling. And before long, I'd hear the gunfire. I'd see the flames of torched shacks shooting up to sear the sky. And I'd know that those corpses had found their scapegoats; that soon, those scapegoats would be needing some vengeance of their own.

Of all the horrors of that Jungle, I think it was the corpses that frightened me the most. Not even jakkals could match them for blood-thirstiness. They were the ones that kept the fires of hate stoked high. It was on account of them that the fighting did not end when the war was won. That war was the great Freedom Struggle, against our racist oppressors. It started as a just campaign. But soon, the power-greedy hijacked the Cause for their own ends. Few in the Jungle feel any sense of liberation now. The Struggle has been over for a long time. Yet we are less free than we ever were. We are slaves to the corpses, to the squabbling warlord packs that fight their territory battles around our homes. But most of all, we are slaves to the scavengers that rule among the ashes of our lives, feeding off our misery. Our weakness makes them stronger. They take what they want from us without resistance, robbing us and raping us as the whim inclines them, knowing we have neither the strength nor the courage to oppose their ruthlessness.

It was, as I have said, a terrible place, that Jondolo of ours. But at least it kept us safe. Because it was so infested, no-one else wanted it. So my grandmother and I were able to live there in peace. I don't know what would have become of us otherwise. We had no money, no family, no way to support ourselves. If it wasn't for the kindness of neighbours, I believe we would have starved.

My grandmother had no strength left for the struggle of living. Once, she was full of fight and courage, a rock that no adversity could crumble. But a sickness had taken root in her the day that my parents were killed. The manner of their death had dealt a mortal blow to her spirit. She was all eaten away inside, like a house that termites had got into. Now there was only the shell left. I was always afraid that the rats would get her. Rats can smell the decay in a person long before death comes.

There were two of them nosing around her when Zach and I entered, twitching their whiskers at her gnarled old feet. They made off in a hurry when they saw the Shadow-slayer. The shadows rolled themselves up and fled out into the sunlight. The corpses unpeeled themselves from the floor. For the first time since I knew it, that Jondolo smelled clean.

I ran to my grandmother, calling 'Gogo, Gogo.'*

She turned her head stiffly to the sound of my voice. She was nearly blind then, but I think it was an inner blindness. Her eyes no longer seemed to focus well on this world.

'Child,' she said, 'Sorrow.' On her lips, my name sounded like a sigh of mourning.

* grandmother

8

'I have brought someone to see you, Gogo,' I told her.

She nodded her head as if she understood. But I saw by the way she looked at Zach that she did not see him.

'Thank you. You are very kind,' she said. 'But I am not hungry. Give it to the child. She needs it more.'

'She thinks you are the neighbours, bringing food,' I explained to Zach.

He nodded and squatted down to take her frail old hands in his.

'Gogo,' he said, 'I am Zach. I have come to see if I can help you. Do you hear me, Gogo?'

'Give it to the child,' she mumbled. 'It is the child who needs it. I am too old to matter.'

'When did she last eat?' Zach asked me. But I couldn't remember. We ate, as I have said, on the charity of the neighbours. When they had food to spare, they fed us. But they had their own hardships, and could not always support the burden of two extra mouths.

'She must have food,' Zach said, looking up to frown at me through his yellow twists of hair. 'Give me the watch, Marinda. Let me go and see what I can find.'

He went out, telling me to wait there for him. I didn't want to, for I was afraid he wouldn't come back. My grandmother turned her head vaguely, calling my name in her dry, frail voice.

'Sorrow,' she sighed, 'Sorrow.'

'Yes, Gogo, I am here.'

But she just shook her head and said again; 'Sorrow, Sorrow.'

9

Her voice had the hollow sound of the corpses I heard moaning in the darkness at night. It frightened me to see her gone so far away. I stood at her shoulder, stroking my fingers through her grizzled hair, humming the Comfort song she used to sing to me when I was troubled. But even that familiar tune could not seem to reach her where she'd gone.

I was glad when Zach came back. He had food with him – a bag of mielie meal, a loaf of bread, a carton of cooked beans. I remember the gentleness with which he coaxed the food into my grandmother's slow, reluctant mouth.

'Eat, Gogo,' I heard him say. 'This food will give you strength. For the child's sake, you must stay strong. A few bites more now. For the child, Gogo. One more for the child.'

I myself needed no such coaxing. In those days, I was always ravenous. I still have not forgotten the taste of those beans, their plumpness bursting under my teeth, releasing their rich, dark flavour into my mouth.

'Slowly, slowly little Cockroach!' Zach laughed. 'Chew before you swallow. If you gulp it down like that, it will only come up again!'

When the time came for him to leave, again I didn't want to let him go. I clung to his legs, beseeching him to take me with him.

'And who will look after your grandmother then?' he said, gently prising my hands apart. 'She will be left here all alone, with no-one to keep her company. You would not want that, would you?'

I shook my head contritely.

'But will you come back then?' I begged him in a whisper.

He gave his promise.

'Soon?' I insisted.

'Yes, little Cockroach, it will be soon,' he smiled. He kissed my worried cheek. And my cheek glowed as though the sun had warmed it. Then he left, taking the day's cheer with him.

I listened forlornly to his footsteps, retreating heat-muffled past our shack. The gloom of the Jondolo closed around me like a stifling pit. The corpses sidled back, grumbling, to their accustomed places. I heard the scuttle of rats, looked down to see their sharp snouts at my feet.

'He won't be back.' they sneered with certainty, tickling my toes with their bold whiskers.

'He will! He gave his promise!'

'What does a promise mean?' they scoffed. I stamped my feet at them.

'You are nothing to him!' they hissed, as they dodged to safer distances. 'Just one more Sorrow in a world that is full of them.'

Desolation filled me at their words. For I feared they spoke the truth.

Three

The rats were wrong however; Zach did keep his promise. He came back two days later – though by then, I had already given up hope. For in my anxious mind, each of those days weighed like a month. The rats' insidious remarks had convinced me I would never see him again.

The weather had not broken, and the afternoon was stifling and unpleasant once more. The shacks broiled so that you could not sit in them. There had been heavy fighting in the night between two Warlord factions, and the smoke of numerous razed shacks hung unmoving in the humid air, blanketing everything in an acrid unreality. I was in the alleyway again, feeding phuthu* crumbs to my cockroach friends. Absorbed in my private talk with them, I did not notice Zach's approach, till their nervy scattering warned me. And looking up, I found his vivid height dazzling my eyes. Happiness kept me dumb-struck. I could not even return his greeting. He hunkered down beside me,

* mielie meal porridge

his face a brown and yellow flower in the fuming air.

'I see you have been conversing with cockroaches again,' he smiled. 'How is their hunger today?'

'A little better,' I told him shyly. 'Only, they are very tired of phuthu now. They would prefer some other food.'

'We will have to see if we can do something about that then.' He patted his bulging pockets. 'In fact, I have here something that might help.'

'What?' I asked expectantly.

His smile tantalized for a moment. 'Magic!' he said, throwing the word like a conjurer to shower its sparkle on the air.

'Would you like to see?'

My nod told him I would indeed.

He reached into his pockets, handed me four small, plain, paper packets. They chuckled dryly when I shook them, hinting at enticing secrets. Eagerly, I ripped them open, expecting . . . I'm not sure what; some rare and technicolour marvel, some edible delight.

'Pips!' I cried indignantly.

'Yes,' Zach said. 'But do you know what happens when you plant those pips?'

I shook my head poutingly, not much caring.

'Magic happens! They grow into food, Marinda. Fat, delicious pumpkins and cabbages, juicy mielies and beans. Your cockroach friends will like this magic, I promise you. They won't have to complain about their hunger anymore.'

The notion intrigued me. I could not imagine

having such plenty to feast on. I could not imagine magic growing here, in this grim and putrid place of death.

We planted the seeds in the narrow strip of ground between our shack and the neighbour's. I waited all week for the magic to reveal itself, for the hard bitter earth to sprout its soft fingers of green, the way Zach said it would. But nothing happened.

'The earth must have eaten them,' I told Zach in disappointment. 'This earth is more hungry even than the cockroaches are. Nothing can grow here.'

'They will grow,' Zach said. His confidence impressed me. It did not allow the possibility of failure. In this place of downtrodden spirits, confidence was a rare phenomenon indeed.

He brought more seeds to plant; but this time, he first fertilized the soil before he planted them. He raided latrines for their smelly nightsoil, ground up old bones and kitchen peelings. He spooned nourishment into that barren soil belly with the same patience and care he had shown towards my grandmother's hunger. Again, I waited eagerly for the promised miracle to happen; and again, was disappointed. This time, it was the appetite of rats that was to blame.

'I hate these rats! They eat up everything!' I groused to Zach. 'They are just like the jakkals. They take whatever we have.'

But Zach still was not discouraged. That's what made him a Slayer of Shadows, you see. He did not flinch from failure. Defeat only strengthened his resolve.

14

He set to work devising rat-traps – simple, cunning contraptions, full of spikes and springs. The rats watched him, laughing, from their secret lairs. The first night that he laid his traps, they skirted them with ease, leaving their excrement contemptuously scattered alongside. But on the second night, when he baited the traps, greed exceeded caution, and one unfortunate was caught. I did not enjoy the sound of its squealing. Mercifully, death soon silenced it. When I went out the next day to look, I found a grisly sight; the corpse with its head firmly caught in the vice of spikes, one bloody eye fixed in staring outrage, its rictus jaws distorted into a snarling grin. Zach did not remove the horror but left it there as a warning to the rest of the tribe. And after that, they gave our seed garden a wide berth.

For the third time, we went through the ritual of planting and waiting. And this time at last, our labour found reward. I watched, entranced, as the first shy heads of green pushed up through the soil, unfurling timidly before my reverent gaze. I watered them with worship and fervour, trudging the long trip to and from the river without complaint. I counted the seedlings daily, shaded them with blankets from the scorching noon-day heat, worried over every blighted leaf.

Others in the vicinity began to take an interest in our garden too, charmed despite themselves by the sight of that tender, trusting growth amid their desolate Jondolos. Neighbours congregated in the cramped space near the vegetable plot, idly chatting as they cooled their eyes with the vision of growing things. Even my grandmother was roused from her strange stupor for a while. She'd sit in the doorway, her vague eyes fixed on the seedlings with peculiar intensity, her head nodding, nodding to itself as though she saw in them the answer to all the world's misfortunes. It was as if what Zach had planted there was more than seeds – as if what grew out of that arid earth was not just vegetables, but something more enduring.

The crop was ripening rapidly in the hot sun. Soon, the first of the fruits would be ready to harvest.

'A few more days,' said Zach, casting a satisfied eye over the bounty. 'Let's give them a little while longer, then they'll be perfect for eating.'

I was in no hurry. I loved those vegetables like my sisters and brothers. I loved to rub my hands over the pumpkins' swollen bellies, and feel the yellow ripeness pulsing inside. I loved to stroke my fingers through the silky hair of the mielies as they nestled inside their sheaths. I loved the intricate whorls of the cabbages, and the slender dance of the beans on their vines. The neighbours, I could see, shared my pleasure. When they stood chatting now beside the garden, their chat was full of expectation. They talked about the leaves of the pumpkin vine, how delicious they tasted when cooked up with mashed pumpkin and phuthu. They said how the fatness of the beans boded well for their tenderness, how the flavour of cabbage could be enhanced by the addition of a curry-flavoured herb they knew. Their laughter bounced between the shack walls like an illicit song.

Laughter was not a common sound in that desperate Jungle of ours. I was afraid of the attention it might attract.

Forebodings, strange and vague, began to trouble my sleep at night. I sensed catastrophe coiled somewhere, ready to loose itself like a judgement against our presumptuous enterprise. But in what form, from where the blow would strike, I couldn't guess.

One sultry midnight, I was roused from troubled dreams by worrying sounds outside our shack – a stealthy commotion that my ears, through my grandmother's snores, could not properly identify. My first thought was that it was Death, come to claim us. I waited in rigid terror for the violent crash of His entrance, the shotgun blast of His breath to sweep us off to oblivion. But it did not come.

The sounds continued – puzzling, unnerving, full of stealthy violence and assault. There were blows, thuds – like heavy bodies dropping down, the sharp snapping of limbs; a continuous tramping passage of feet to and fro, to and fro. Till finally, they ceased, leaving behind them unenlightening silence.

I lay for the rest of that night in suspense, too fearful to sleep. It wasn't until morning that I found the courage to leave my bed and look outside. I think I knew what I was going to find; but still, the discovery shocked me.

Lit by the blood of dawn, I saw my devastated garden. It lay littered with the wreckage of itself, battered and blasted as though by some relentless storm. Thieves had carried off the vegetables; but that was not all they'd done. They'd laid waste there – deliberately, spitefully. Every plant had been uprooted, stems hacked and slashed, foliage trampled into the ground. Not one survivor had escaped the carnage. The viciousness of these thieves hinted strongly to me of jakkal influence.

An offensive stench drew my eyes to a closer perusal. And I saw there the message that had been left for me to see. It was a pile of human excrement, malevolently coiled amid the wreckage, where eyes could not miss its contemptuous innuendo. 'Hope mocks the slave,' it said.

I cried for days over my ruined garden, at the thought of the untender hands that had invaded there. It felt to me as if some deeper violation had occurred; I think I was not the only one who felt that way. We did not see much of the neighbours from then on. There was no more congenial gossiping in the sunlight, no more bold laughter. They kept to themselves, allowing the grimness of life to engulf them again, bearing their hardships separately, as we did ours. My grandmother retreated back into her far-away distance, more lost to this world than ever. It was left to Zach to be my comforter.

'Don't cry – don't cry, little sister,' he said. 'We'll plant another garden. We'll grow an even better crop of vegetables. And this time, I'll make sure that nobody dares to steal them from us!'

His words only made me sob the harder, however.

I did not weep only for my lost garden, you see,

but for the inevitability of its loss. For it seemed to me that in some subtle way, I had called the disaster down on my own head. I had allowed myself to be seduced by confidence. I had dared to forget the incontrovertible credo that is branded indelibly into every Jungle-dweller's soul:

'Hope for nothing. Strive for nothing. Learn to love nothing. For as surely as there are shadows, of all you value shall you be bereft.'

Four

I have always liked the darkness better than the day. I don't know why. Night is the time of danger in our Jungle, the time of predators and corpses. But night is also the time of the sky. Often, when I couldn't sleep for the shadows, when the sounds of dying and burning kept me awake, I would creep outside, and hide myself in a dark spot, and wait for the sky to sweep me away. The sky is a wonderful place to go wandering. It's clean there, free, full of peace. There are no scavengers, no rats to bother you. Nothing but silence and stars and space. Some nights, the moon would come visiting, white and sharp, like a snake's tooth; or round and rich and yellow, like something you could eat. I loved the soundless race of the clouds on windy nights, the way the whole sky seemed to surge with swift, restless motion. I loved the giddy feeling as I lay back under the dark streaming and let its current catch me. I'd see the stars, adrift on their deep sea, so bright and far – higher than everything. I'd watch them sail on past me – off to a better place, I was certain, far from the Jungle's ugliness. And every cell of my being would yearn for them to take me too.

The night they came to kill my parents, it was the sky that saved me. I was outside, sailing with the stars, when the jakkals broke into my house. And so I was spared the fate that snared the rest of my household. The first I knew of what was happening, was when I saw the stars begin to dribble blood. The sky cracked with a terrible sharp thunder – and I thought in my confusion that it had shattered itself and was about to fall down on my head. I remember my grandmother running bloodstained from the house with her eyes full of terror, sweeping me up and carrying me off into the veld. I remember that it took our house a long time to die, that I wept for its agony as I watched the flames consume it. I didn't know then that my father and brothers were still inside it. The jakkals had shot them. They gave no reason. They were drunk, I think, and simply wanting some amusement. Guns are a law unto themselves in our Jungle. They speak when they want to speak, caring nothing about justice. My mother was less fortunate. She was still alive when the jakkals burned her. They said she was a witch. They said she ate the hearts of young girls and kept them as zombie slaves in her back yard. They put a burning tyre around her neck and laughed at her agony as her flesh melted into her bones. They knew, of course, that it was lies. My mother was no witch. She had a healing gift, that's all. She liked to help people. It was that goodness in her that offended them. Excrement loves only its own smell. The shadow detests the Slayer.

After the calamitous end to our vegetable garden, I was afraid that Zach would lose interest in our troubles. But he continued to visit us regularly, always with some sustaining gift of food – still determined, you see, to save us from our starvation. I lived for his visits, though they were never frequent enough for me. On the days when he did not come, I'd sulk listlessly in the Jondolo, finding purpose in nothing. Sharing grumbles with the cockroaches as they scavenged among the rat droppings for food. I always knew, somehow, when his arrival was imminent. My heart would start to beat erratically. I'd feel a breathless expectation grip me. My ears would strain across the distance, imagining they heard the approaching creak of his bicycle – an old machine he had recently purchased – crossing the brown emptiness of veld that bordered the Jungle, labouring through the first uneven lanes. I'd go racing through the alleyways in search of him, too keyed up to pay heed to the menace of scavengers, throwing myself at him like a wild thing when I finally came upon him.

'How did you know I was coming, Marinda? Which bird told you?' he would ask me, laughing and amazed. But I could never tell him how I knew, for it was a mystery even to me.

Ever since I can remember, it has been this way with me. I have heard things, seen things, sensed things in a way that is different to other people. I can tell the sickness in a plant before it starts to wither. I can see the sickness in a person too. I can look into their eyes and see disease shadowed there. I can smell the hatred that corrodes the soul. There

22

are faces that I can't bear to look into at all, for what lies behind them is too repellent – the souls all eaten away with shadows, great gangrenous chunks dropping off them, like leprous fingers. Sometimes, it is a curse to be gifted with too much acuity of vision. For underneath its skin, the world is a very black and awful place.

It could not fail to be apparent to Zach right from the first that I was not as other children were. Yet he wasn't unnerved by my oddity as most were. If anything, it made him more tender towards me – as if I was some rare, fey creature that the world's coarseness might bruise. It is not easy to explain the bond that grew between us.

I have already explained the compelling attraction he held for me. But what drew him to me is not so obvious. I think it was my need that touched him. There was a deep tenderness in him towards all defenceless things. Suffering drew him irresistibly – he could not turn his back on it. He had the healer's need to root out pain and make the injured whole again. In that, he was like my mother. Only his healing took a different form. His province was the mind; his skill, to set caged spirits free. He hated to see young souls trapped in the squalor of their circumstance. He wanted to plant dreams inside them, to help them reach for better things. That was what had brought him to the vicinity of our Jungle.

He had come to teach at the school down in the valley, where children from the neighbouring township went. We of the Jungle were supposed to attend it too. But most of us did not have the energy for the daily excursion. It was a long walk from our Jungle to that school, across the wide stretch of open veld, down steep hillsides and across more veld, to the edge of the industrial flats, where the school was situated.

My grandmother took me there once, to silence my insistent nagging. But the arduousness of the journey defeated us both. I remember sitting bewildered in the classroom, sandwiched amid an overflow of other small bodies, watching the teacher open and close her mouth. Words were coming out of it, but I couldn't hear them. I only saw the shapes they made. They looked like food to me – fat loaves of bread and twisting sausage snakes, scones and apples and frothing streams of milk. I watched them whirling round and round the classroom, dodging in and out between the heads of the children. Eventually I remember, I grew so giddy that I fell off my seat. The other children laughed, and their laughter felt like small, sharp beaks, jabbing at me. I ran out of the classroom on that occasion, and couldn't be persuaded to return.

That was my first and only experience of school, till Zach came. When I found out that he was teaching there, my interest was renewed. Every so often, when strength permitted, I'd trudge the long trudge there, usually arriving midway through the first lesson of the morning. I'd creep into the room where Zach was teaching and install myself unnoticed, like a little burrowing mouse, in a back corner behind the desks. Zach taught the senior classes – far too advanced for me. But I wasn't troubled by that. So long as I could be where he was, I was content. I liked to watch his yellow head moving against the blackboard, to see his face light up with the animation of his subject. When his mouth spoke, it wasn't food that came out, but colours and poetry. I'd sit there, drenched in the vividness, my mind not always understanding the complexities of what I heard, yet some part of me deeply stirred.

There was one poem in particular that I remember. It was called The Making of A Servant.* It told the story of a young, proud ox being broken to the yoke. This poem distressed me unbearably. Its simple images evoked so eloquently the bitter impotence of servitude, the brutal subordination of the will to debasing tyranny. It seemed to me that the pain of that young ox was my pain too; but not only mine. In his anguished bellows, I heard the despairing cry of all fettered souls, who had known the choking rope.

When the lesson was over that day, I did not leave as usual when the other children did, but stayed in my corner, too overcome to move. Zach discovered me there, weeping my tragic streams of tears.

'Marinda! What are you doing here? Why are you crying like that – tell me! Has something happened?'

But all I could do was sob incoherently, 'The Ox – the Ox!'

'The Ox? Ah, the one in the poem you mean! Is that what's upset you? You were here for the lesson?'

* The Making Of A Servant – by J J R Jolobe

25

I nodded, spraying him with my tears.

'But it's only a poem, silly child!' he laughed at me tenderly. 'There is no need to let it upset you like this. That Ox is only a story ox – he doesn't really exist. He's a symbol, just a symbol. Can you understand that?'

I could not be so easily consoled, however. For to me, the Ox was very real. Every day, in countless Jungle faces, I saw his despairing eyes looking out at me. I watched his proud, brave spirit grow trembling and crushed as the yoke choked tighter, and the punishing blows rained down.

The day that I turned nine, Zach was the only one who knew or cared. It was a Saturday, I remember, and he came to visit me in the morning, bringing my birthday gift – a pair of sandals made from tyre rubber, the kind the people call im'badada. They were at least two sizes too big for me, and I flapped in them like an unsteady crow. But they made me feel like the queen of everything. It was a long time since I had had any shoes to wear at all. I paraded in them with a swagger that made Zach laugh. I tried to show them off to my grandmother too. But she was far gone these days, retreated deep into her papery carapace, where voices seldom reached her. Zach did his best to make up for her absence.

'Now we must decide what we are going to do with our day,' he said to me briskly. 'Since it's your birthday, Marinda, you must choose.'

'Can I choose anything?' I asked, delighted at the prospect. He smiled his Shadow-slayer's smile at me. 'The day is yours!'

26

I thought about my choice, feeling rich as royalty with such a feast of possibilities before me. I nibbled at each one, tasting and discarding, taking my time.

'I think that I would like to see some birds,' I finally announced.

'Birds?' Zach echoed, somewhat mystified.

'Yes. It is a very long time since I have seen any birds,' I told him. 'There used to be some here once. But the people caught them all for food.'

Zach looked at me in silence for a moment. 'All right, little Cockroach,' he said, hugging me to him warmly. 'You can have your wish. It so happens that I know a place where a lot of birds are. I think you will like it there.'

He took me on his bicycle, sitting on the crossbar in front of him, balanced back against his chest. The bicycle went slowly with its double load. But it felt to me like we were flying. Zach sang in my ear and the wind lifted us up and carried us across the veld as though we were nothing. A cobra lay across our path, dry brown against the dry brown grass. But I wasn't afraid of it, for I saw it intended us no harm. It turned its flat, deadly head to watch as we flew past it, hissing its approval of our escape.

I looked back once. And I saw the Jungle's ugly shadow squatting behind us, the fumes of excrement and decomposing corpses rising up to shroud it like poisoned smoke. And the sight of its hideousness was terrible to me, even from that distance.

Five

It took us almost an hour to reach the place where the birds were. It was a small patch of bushy forest on the bend of the river, surrounded by veld and sky. The sight of so much green entranced me so that I could hardly speak. The soaring height of the trees made me dizzy. Birds flew like bright bolts of energy between the canopies, leaving trails of glittering colour where they passed. Their air-born grace filled me with indescribable joy. I had forgotten how extraordinary their flight was, how their wings could set me free.

Zach smiled at my dumbfounded silence. 'Well, little sister? Will this place do? Are there birds enough for you here?'

I could only nod, too overwhelmed to speak. Wherever I turned, I saw magic and wonder. I saw colours and shining and little miracles. Butterflies danced at my shoulder. Everything here seemed to be dancing – the sky, the trees, the river, the day. A great bursting happiness inflated my heart. I could not remember when last I had felt so free.

We sat on the bank of the river, cooling our feet

in its murky brown current. Dragonflies trembled in the bars of sunlight and swallows skimmed by like swift arrows, dipping their breasts to the water, then twisting up in effortless spirals to brush the sky.

Zach told me the story of the river, how it was born in a high place in the stone mountains, very far away, how it spent its whole life wandering, searching everywhere for its one true love, the sea.

'Poor river,' I said. 'How lonely he must be! Does he ever find this sea?'

'Oh yes,' Zach reassured me. 'True love is always rewarded in the end. In fact, they are not so very far away from each other now. She lives in that direction.' His hand showed me.

'What is she like, this sea? Have you ever seen her?' I asked him curiously.

He nodded. 'I know her well. The village where I lived when I was a child is right beside the sea.'

'Are there rats there?'

'No, no rats, only cockroaches,' he smiled.

'Then I would like to go there someday. I would like to see this sea for myself.'

'She is very beautiful,' Zach said, his yellow eyes full of dreams in the sunlight. 'There is nothing like her in all the world. She is so big that only the sky can see all of her. So blue, that even the sun's eyes are dazzled. Sometimes, she shines with a thousand lights, like shoals of silver fishes darting through her. And she is very restless, waiting for her love the river to arrive. Sighing and tossing and moaning to herself all day and night long.'

The hours of our freedom passed very pleasantly. We watched birds, explored the river, collecting treasures of pebbles and feathers and pods that we found along the way. Zach caught a fish for our lunch – I don't know how he did it. He baited the water with grubs to lure them, then netted one in his shirt as it surfaced beside him. I was sorry to be the cause of its death. I did not like the desperation of its agile body as Zach fought to hold it, or to watch its eyes glaze over when he wrenched its head. But hunger was sharper than my pity. And I was glad enough to eat it when the time came.

We cooked it in an oven of stones, garnished with wild mushrooms and some lemon-scented leaf that Zach found. I thought it the most delicious meal I had ever tasted. For it was flavoured with clean air and wind-shadow, with the pulsating songs of birds – and the sweeter relish of Zach's presence beside me.

Afterwards, replete and drowsy, we lay curled together in the swaying shade of the trees, our ears lulled by their rustling music, at peace and content. I felt my happiness pulsing through my body like a deep drumbeat, matched to the rhythm of Zach's heart against my back. I felt his breath warming the skin of my shoulders, his arms curled round my body like a protective cocoon. And I lay there, still and quiet in the silky centre, feeling the changing of something inside me, feeling myself slowly transformed out of my thin and awkward ugliness, into something wonderful.

Six

My grandmother died that autumn. She simply stopped breathing one night. The frail flutter of her spirit finally went out, leaving the shell of her body untenanted. I sat alone with her corpse all through the long hours of darkness, too afraid to leave and go for help in case the rats began to feed on her. I remember that I felt very much alone.

'I have no-one in the world now,' I said to Zach when he came the next day, weeping my forlorn tears onto his shoulder.

'You have me,' he told me quietly. His arms embraced me tightly. 'You have me, little sister. I'll look after you. You don't need to worry.'

He took me to live with him in his house, with him and his woman, Naomi. His house was small – a single-roomed hut that he had built himself out of earth and grass thatch. It stood on its own in the veld, perched on the crest of the hill that led down to the valley where the school was. It had its own supply of water, drawn from the borehole tank outside. This made it seem a very rich house to me. I liked it much better there than in my Jondolo. It was clean and neat inside, with mats of woven grass and pieces of coloured cloth at the windows. There was no stink of corpses there, no rats. At first, this felt very strange to me. I was so used to the smell of shadows by then – it felt as if one of my senses was missing. I remember the first night, waking in terror from nightmares, to find Zach on his knees beside me.

'What? What is it, little sister? What's frightening you?' he asked. But all I could stammer was, 'The shadows . . . the shadows . . . !'

'What shadows? There are no shadows here,' he soothed. 'I will keep you safe from any shadows. Don't be afraid,' he said. He held me and talked to me until my trembling lessened. His voice was like a warm fire in the darkness. His Shadowslayer's strength was very comforting.

'Would you like me to tell you a story?' he asked me presently, yawning against my head. I whispered yes, the one about the river and the sea. So he told it to me again, his voice like the river itself, soothing and steady. I closed my eyes and let its current take me, away through the world to the place of colours and dreams. I saw the vast shining of the blue-black water, with the red moon rising out of it and the numerous stars shining over it. I saw the black, sleek bodies of the long-nosed, legless creatures that cleaved through it. And the huge, foam-topped water mountains lifting like restless dragons, to curl and crash and rise again in their endless green-backed dance. I cannot say why those images were so comforting to me. They freed me in the same way that the flight of birds did. They were sanctuary from the Jungle's ugliness. They were proof that its cruel tentacles did not reach everywhere.

I knew though, that its reach was long. And for that reason I could not rejoice whole-heartedly in the improvement of my fortunes. Nightmares continued to trouble me. I was continually bracing myself for calamity, for the demolishing blow. For I knew better than anyone, the spite of shadows. Zach's house was a source of great uneasiness for me. I saw how it stood, so unaware and virginal, smiling its clean-breathed smile at the Jungle's ugliness. I felt the Jungle's salivating thoughts as it stared back across the veld towards us; imagined its sly pseudopodic creep across the separating distance – shack by shack, closer, closer. I feared for that house – and for us who lived there. Shadows loathe the unblemished thing. For that, they reserve a special despoilation.

I sought the advice of my good friends, the cockroaches. What they had to say was simple and sound.

'The poison of snakes makes the best anti-venom,' they told me. At first, I did not altogether understand their implication. But as I thought about it, the meaning became clear.

'What this house needs is the talisman of corpses,' I decided.

Wasting no time, I went off at once to visit my old Jondolo. I didn't mind the long walk there at all. I was even singing a little, I remember – but softly, lest my happiness attract the evil attention of Spite. It felt very strange to step through the familiar doorway and find all waiting there just as I'd left it, as if I'd never left at all. The reek of the place seemed more offensive than ever. But I drank it in almost fondly, my nostrils clogged with memory. The corpses sat up to stare at me with their hideous eyes, reproaching me for my desertion. My grandmother was with them, I noticed. But her gaze was kindly.

'The rat is the embodiment of foulness,' she told me – which I knew already. 'There is no stink like theirs.'

There was a brace of them lurking under the rotting pile of fallen planks in the corner. I lured them out with the bait of dead dog brains I'd brought, which I knew they love especially.

'Well look, it is our Prodigal,' they sneered, as they steeped their snouts in my gory offering. 'We knew you would be back. Sorrow belongs here.'

'I am not Sorrow anymore. I am Marinda now,' I told them haughtily, watching their snuffling greed with loathing.

'What difference does a name make? You are still a slave to shadows. We will keep your corner warm,' they hissed in spite. 'You will be back!'

Their gloating was cut short by the sound of spiked jaws snapping. From the baited rubbish pile where I'd laid my rat-trap ambush, came a cacophony of outraged squeals. Unfortunately this victim, though firmly caught, was very much alive still. I had to help its death along myself with the kitchen knife I'd brought for the purpose. It was a very gruesome business. And despite my detestation for the creatures, I almost lacked the resolve to see it through. But finally it was over, and I had my rat corpse, oozing gory malevolence from every pore.

I carried it back to Zach's house in triumph, and buried it that night in a secret ritual, in a shallow, uncovered grave scraped at the corner of the hut. By the next morning already, the talisman had begun to work. I detected with satisfaction the black vapours of the corpse, oozing out around the hut's foundations, enveloping it in protective stench. Zach and Naomi could not fail to detect it too.

'What is that bad smell? There is a terrible smell around this house today!' I heard Naomi complaining. 'It smells like something has died here. Like a dead rat somewhere.'

'It does smell like dead rats,' Zach frowned. 'Perhaps it's outside.'

'There's a dead dog in the veld,' I told him, running quickly to forestall his search. 'I saw it yesterday, not far from here. It's that smell that we're smelling.'

I took him to the place. And it was true, that dog did smell very bad. Zach dug a deep hole and buried the remains. But of course, that did not help the stink in the house. Corrupting rat flesh has an odour like nothing else on earth. It grew so bad, that at last even I couldn't stand it, and was forced to fill the grave in. After that, we were all able to sleep better at night.

I think though, that Naomi suspected something. Whether she heard me at work with the spade in the darkness, I can't say. But for a while, I found myself watched far too closely for my liking. Her mistrustful gaze followed me everywhere. And it seemed I couldn't do anything without her coming over to check what I was up to.

Seven

I have thought often that it could not have been easy for Naomi, to be landed with me, the strange invader in her home. She was hardly more than a child herself at that time – not so much in age, as in unworldliness. She lacked the tough resilience of those born to the Jungle streets. Life had not yet laid its grubby fingers on her. There was an endearing softness about her, almost a defenceless air. I think it was that that made Zach love her. For she stirred the protector in him.

I thought her very beautiful. She had the bearing of a king's daughter, the grace of colts in her walk. She had lovely almond brown eyes, a high smooth forehead, a wide, sweet mouth. I liked Naomi, and I greatly admired her also. And it saddened me to know that she did not reciprocate my liking. Oh, she was kind enough to me in her way. But she didn't *like* me. I always felt with her like the stray that I was, an interloper to be tolerated, but not loved. My strangeness made her uneasy, I think. It unnerved her for instance, to find me talking to cockroaches. Or running in my prescient

way to fling the door open for Zach's home-
coming – before he was even within sight of the
hut. Once, she caught me sawing off some strands
of his hair as he lay sleeping. I wanted them for an
amulet I was making. But my explanation didn't
pacify her.

Even then, even in those early days, she was a
little afraid of me, I think. She took me for a
witch-child, full of dark intentions. And my odd
looks didn't help matters at all. When her eyes
looked at me, I saw my ugliness reflected there.
For undoubtedly, I was ugly at that time. Hunger
had warped me and stunted me. My hair was
sparse and rust-coloured from Kwashiorkor.* My
face seemed to be all eyes. My face was the face of
sorrow. And that filled me with a bottomless regret. For I longed more than anything to cast off
the curse of that name, to be transformed in reality
into Marinda. Only Zach made me feel that such a
thing was possible. When I looked into his eyes, I
saw the reflection of what I wanted to be. I saw
the creature inside the ugly chrysalis – the butterfly
still to emerge.

Living under the same roof as Zach was a source
of deep satisfaction to me. It made me very content to be able to eat my meals with him each day,
to sleep at night within sound of his breathing, to
wake in the morning to the sight of his yellow hair
warming the room. I didn't begrudge Naomi her
claims on him. For I knew at some deep level that
his love for her in no way diminished the bond he
shared with me. At night, as I lay on my mat in

* Kwashiorkor = malnutrition

the corner, the sounds of their love-making would lull me to sleep. I would drift off on the tides of their quickened breathing, carried into a sleep that was blissfully free of the vengeful moans of corpses. Sometimes from our hut, we would hear the sharp snarl of the Jungle guns reverberating across the veld towards us. But their threat seemed far away from this life, from this charmed hut.

I had started going regularly to school now. For Zach insisted.

'The world has no pity for the ignorant and poor, Marinda,' he told me. 'You do not want to have to live in a snakepit like that one all your life, do you?' He was referring of course to the Jungle.

I shook my head with feeling.

'Then you must seize your chance while you still have it. You must acquire an education. For knowledge gives you skills to barter for a better life.'

He no longer indulged my presence in his classes either, but insisted I attend my own, to learn what was appropriate for my age-group.

For many weeks, this banishment was a source of great misery to me. I was not interested in the lessons for my age-group. I only wanted to hear what Zach had to teach. The formal structure of the classes did not suit my temperament at all. I felt trapped in my desk, my mind assaulted by the boring repetition of things that made no sense to me. The teacher, I know, thought me defective. She laboured in vain to help me catch up the work I'd missed. My attention fluttered like a moth at a window. Teaching me to read was a torture for us both. When I stared at the black letters on their white cards, I saw shapes without meaning. My brain could not connect them to anything real in the world. I shed many tears of despair at my obtuseness. And so too did the teacher, I think, in her private moments.

The attitude of my classmates did not help my troubles either. My oddness and my late arrival in their midst conspired to make me an outcast in their eyes. Because of my smallness, I was an easy target for their bullying. They nicknamed me the Tokolosh, which is a kind of ugly, malevolent imp much feared in my part of the world. Their hurtful rejection of me only served to make me cling more desperately to Zach. For it seemed to me that he was my only refuge in a friendless world.

I was – I admit it – very possessive of my Shadow-slayer in those early months. I could scarcely bear to let him out of my sight at all. I followed him everywhere, dogging his footsteps like a faithful shadow, like a small, determined bodyguard. My attachment was in part, I think, based on my fear of losing him. I was deeply haunted by the dread that he would be snatched away from me – as so much else that I loved had been snatched away. I still felt the Jungle's shadow breathing over my shoulder, still lived in daily expectation of its treachery. I hated to let Zach go in there without me. He had scant regard for its dangers, no inkling of the ambushes that waited there. He did not know how violence could ignite out of the air and strike you down without reason or warning. He did not see the way the jakkal gangs fastened their plotting eyes on him. They had no liking for this bold new flower in their territory. It did not suit them to have a Shadow-slayer at work there, encouraging the spirits of the people, upsetting the convenient balance of things.

I felt the little acrid draughts of their hatred, following us as we trundled down the narrow lanes on Zach's old bicycle. I was continually bracing myself for the confrontation I was sure must come. But how to stop Zach from going in there, I didn't know. That great open sore of need and suffering on our doorstep drew him like a magnet. He seemed to hold himself personally responsible for the alleviation of its ills. His bicycle was always laden with food parcels for the hungry. He was always adopting some destitute family under his wing, as once he had adopted us. The hunger of children bothered him particularly. Almost as much, he worried over their malnourished minds.

He tried to start a school for them, holding it on Saturday mornings, on a plot of disused ground filled with the blackened skeletons of burned-down shacks. It didn't last long however, this school. Jakkals closed it down. A pack of them appeared one day, strolling up out of the grimy morning to cast their shadows over the proceedings.

'We do not recall giving you permission to hold your school here, Mr Schoolmaster,' they said to Zach, flashing their switchblade smiles towards him menacingly. 'This ground is not your ground. You must pay us if you want the use of it.'

'It is not your ground either,' Zach said, yellow

anger flaring in his eyes. 'And you are disrupting our lesson. So please leave.'

You can see that he was not used to the authority of jakkals. He did not fully understand at that stage who he was dealing with. He thought that to stand up to bullies was the way to deflate their power. I trembled for him as they came towards him, kicking a path through the cringing children. In the blank fields of their sunglasses, I saw his tiny bright-haired image reflected – a flame too easily extinguished.

'You do not seem to understand the way things work here, Friend,' their spokesman told him, scratching at his dreadlocks with the curving red nail of his little finger. All the jakkals had them, these bloody talons. It was the insignia they affected.

'Since you are new here, we will explain it to you. Listen carefully. In this place, all ground belongs to us. We own everything. Even the people. If you want to do anything, you must first consult with us. That is how it works here. You will save a lot of pain by remembering that.'

'Must I defecate also only when you say so?' said Zach derisively. The jakkals were not pleased by that answer. Even behind their sunglasses, I could see the anger that inflamed their eyes – how they longed to grind their bootheels into the face of this Upstart, and impress their lessons of respect on him in ways he would never forget. But his confidence disconcerted them. For it seemed to confirm what his hair hinted at, some immunity he had access to that was better not trifled with.

Even the boldest of jakkals will hesitate to lay his hands on a Sorcerer. Madness, the wasting disease, evil spirits – these are only a few of the afflictions that Wizards can supposedly invoke upon a person's life. Belief in such things runs very deep in our Jungle.

So they chose safer targets to unleash their wrath on. Turning from Zach, they advanced instead upon the frightened children.

'This school is closed!' they snarled at them. 'Go home now – all of you. Scram – quickly! It will be very bad for any of you that we catch here in future.'

To drive their point home, they laid about them with boots and fists, till the whole crowd fled in terror. They saw right from the first, you see, that the way to get at Zach was through pain to others. There are more ways than one to bring a troublesome dog to heel.

That was Zach's first experience of jakkal viciousness. And it shocked him, I could see. The casual brutality of their assault against the children outraged him deeply; his own impotence in the face of it left a very bitter taste in his mouth. I myself, however, could only feel relief that things had not gone a different way. Another time, I knew we might not be so lucky; once jakkal knives are out, there's no telling what they'll stop at. Even Zach's hair might not be able to safeguard him should they be provoked – or drunk – enough.

I gave him the amulet I had been working on – a childish charm, but imbued with all the magical potency my will could wish on it. It was made from the fleshy, warty pod of the Toad Tree, which I had filled with a careful recipe of things; butterfly wings and bird feathers for luck, the bright strands cut from Zach's hair; a few drops of my own blood, mixed with a virulent brew of berry and insect poisons, for bite.

Zach seemed more amused than impressed when I handed him the offering, though he took it with good grace.

'It is a talisman. To protect you from your enemies.' I told him earnestly. 'There is magic in it. Keep it on you always. Never be without it.'

'I have no enemies,' he smiled. 'But thank you Marinda. I will treasure this all the same.'

He hung the ugly thing around his neck on a leather thong. For he could see it meant a lot to me that he should wear it. Naomi though, was much less tolerant towards my gift. I don't know what it was about that amulet that bothered her so much. But she disliked it intensely. I heard her whispering at night when she and Zach lay together.

'Why do you wear this horrible thing? Take it off, Zach! It's so ugly. It bruises me. I don't sleep well when you wear it. Take it off Zach, take it off!'

To humour her, he did. But every morning, when I checked, I'd see it round his neck again, its outline bulging up reassuringly beneath his shirt. And this was a great relief to me.

Eight

It was soon after my tenth birthday, when I had been living in Zach's house for almost a year, that a new arrival came to join our oddly-assorted family. This was an old skeletal mule that Zach and I had discovered on one of our visits to the Jungle. We'd found her tethered to some destitute family's shack – all bones and hanging skin and misery. She was in truly pitiful condition, riddled with sores and mange and parasites, so weak she could scarcely make the journey back to our hut. She'd been surviving, it seemed, on nothing but vegetable peelings and phuthu scrapings, which was all the family could spare to feed her. Zach gave her into my charge – a responsibility I eagerly accepted. For one look at this poor, emaciated wreck had made me her willing slave.

I nursed her devotedly, stayed awake through the night to feed her her small, regular allotments of invalid's gruel. I treated her mange and in-festations with the smelly concoctions that the Jungle herbalists prescribed. I endured, without rancour, her sour temper and her patent lack of gratitude. For she was, in truth, a very mean-spirited old nag. Her sufferings had left her with a grudge against humanity that no amount of kindness could dispell. She had a vicious sidekick, which she used with devastating effect. She would eat the apple from your hand – then promptly nip you for your pains. The one and only time I tried to mount her, she unseated me with a violence that left me bruised for days. Yet none of this detracted in any way from her charm for me. If anything, it only made me love her more. I knew very well what it was to be the world's misfit. I felt towards her the deep affinity of one outcast for another.

I called her Cockroach, because of her brown coat – and her constant complaining, which reminded me of those old friends of mine. She had a bray that could raise the roof off the hut. Its doleful tone was so redolent of the world's injustice that it never failed to bring tears to my eyes. Other members of the household found it less endearing, however; particularly when startled from their sleep by a high-pitched blast of it directly under the window at night.

Naomi's nerves were considerably strained. She took to this new foundling even less than she had taken to me; to be fair, in this case too she had good reason. Even I, who loved Cockroach so, had to admit that she was not an easy presence to live with. Her loud bray and her grudging temper were not her only faults. Her intimate acquaintance with starvation had left her with an undiscriminating appetite. Books, food meant for our supper, the curtains, shoes – all was grist to the mill of her tough yellow teeth. She had a particular predilection for Naomi's things. It was not at all unusual for me to arrive back from school to find Naomi ranting and in tears over some shredded garment, the veld littered with missiles, and Cockroach nowhere to be seen.

Naturally, I would be forced to take my darling's part in the dispute. Caring nothing for Naomi's pain, my sole concern would be the effect that her harsh treatment might have had on my beloved's fragile, brutalized spirit. I'd run off tearfully in search of her and lure her home again with much coaxing; mollifying her agitated nerves with some stolen treat of bread or pumpkin meant for our supper. None of which improved my relations with Naomi in any way.

Once, driven to the limits by some particular offence of Cockroach's, Naomi threatened to sell her to the Jungle butchers. My shrieking hysteria at the notion startled us both. I threatened Naomi with lightning – death – the wasting disease; every horrible thing I could think of. Where these curses came from, I have no idea. But they stayed between us for a long time.

In spite of her good intentions, Naomi's dislike of me had not subsided over the months. As my unwanted presence in her life became more entrenched, so it seemed to grow more difficult for her to keep her antipathy hidden. I do not mean to imply that she was unkind to me – for she wasn't. She took care of me scrupulously, attended to my physical needs without complaint; cooked for me, deloused my hair, sewed my clothes. But there remained a rejecting coldness in her manner towards me that she couldn't disguise. I was the cuckoo child in her nest, and she just couldn't love me.

I know she longed for children of her own. But she could not fall pregnant. I felt that in some peculiar way, she held me to blame for her barrenness, as if my presence brought some jinx to her life. Part of her trouble, I suspect, was simple loneliness. All day, while Zach and I were off together on our various business at the school or in the Jungle, she was left to brood with her thoughts alone. Our isolated hut in the veld must sometimes have seemed a type of purgatory to her. For she had a gregarious nature, and would have been far happier in the thick of city or township, with neighbours to gossip with and the convenient luxuries of electricity and television to sweeten the drudgery of the days. In this, as in so many things, she and Zach were very opposite. To him, our small and spartan hut in the veld was happiness epitomized. He loved, as I did, its peace and privacy, the empty veld around it, its unobstructed views of sky.

At night, the two of us would often sit out in the darkness together, admiring the black enigma above us, united in our awe. Zach knew the names of all the major constellations. He taught me the mythology of the sky. I listened, spellbound, to his stories of jealous gods and heroic mortals. Looking up, I'd see the glittering reality of their figures fixed in the night.

Sometimes, when the mood took him, he'd play his violin for me – an old brown fiddle that once had belonged to his father, he said. I loved the sound of that fiddle more than anything. Its sweet, deep voice always made me think of purple water. The tunes Zach played on it had a disturbing, haunting beauty to them. Naomi found them too sad. But for me, their dark sorrow held the allure of recognition – as if they gave voice to some melancholy strain inside myself. I'd watch Zach with his eyes half closed, his bright shaggy head bent lovingly close to the instrument. And I'd feel a feeling stirring in me impossible to explain. The intensity of the music would flow through my body like unbearable yearning. I'd watch the motions of Zach's hands, the deft and tender stroking of his bow against the strings. And it would feel, in a strange way, as if it was from my body that he drew the music; as if I was the violin, and the sweet, vibrating stream of sound poured out of me.

Sometimes, when the intensity of emotion grew too much for me, I'd have to jump up and dance the devils away. I'd spin and whirl and leap in un-caring abandonment; dipping, arching, surging like a seatide this way and that. Zach's head would lift to watch me while his hands continued to play me. And it would be as if the two of us were joined in the same spell, the same dream; adrift in a star-strewn universe of longing and pain.

Nine

Years passed, flowing by hardly noticed. Nothing major befell us in that time. Catastrophe did not seek us out. Whether it was the rat corpse under the hut that we had to thank for our immunity, or whether the Jungle was simply biding its time, saving itself for some particular cruelty, was hard to know. I strongly feared the latter. I knew, deep inside me, that I was still a slave to shadows. Yet I allowed myself to be lulled by the reprieve all the same. I stopped anticipating doom with every sunrise, learnt to be more trusting of good fortune. That isn't to say that life was free of worries during this period. The cold war between Zach and the jakkals continued to be a source of great concern to me. Since their clash over the school, there had been no more open confrontations between them. But beneath the surface, hostilities simmered. And I was always unconsciously bracing myself for the circumstances that would light the fuse.

Birthdays came and went. And before I knew it, I wasn't a child any longer, but fourteen. The chrysalis had at last discharged its promise. I was straighter, taller, with well-developed breasts and flesh on my bones. My face was not beautiful the way Naomi's was. But something in my look was arresting to people. Zach had told me that.

'You have haunting eyes, Marinda,' he said to me once, 'Those beautiful eyes of yours are going to break many hearts one day.'

His words, though lightly said, were deeply pleasing to me, for I wanted above all things to know that Zach found my looks appealing. But at the same time, they saddened me. For it struck me very forcibly then that there was only one heart in the world that I wanted to have power over. And that one was taboo to me.

The intimacy of our living arrangements had become an increasing trial to me. Zach's nearness no longer contented me, but affected me with bewildering yearnings. My body seemed full of strange restlessness. The most casual of Zach's affectionate touches could set off powerful chain reactions that left me shaken and dismayed in ways I did not understand. The sight of him and Naomi embracing wracked me with guilty jealousy. At night, as I lay lonely in my corner, the sounds of their love-making no longer lulled me, but filled me with strange burning.

Zach, I am certain, had no idea of the changed nature of my feelings for him. To him, I was still the little sister, and my love for him was the innocent love of a child. But Naomi knew. I saw it in the brooding cast of her eyes when she looked at me, in the subtle way she interposed herself between her man and me at every chance. The early friction between us developed into a full-blown, mutual enmity. Sometimes, the air crackled so fiercely with our hostility that it felt like a brewing storm. But Zach detected none of it. We were careful to keep our feelings hidden from him, each of us fearing, I think, to make him choose between us; lest his choice favour the other.

Winter came. And it was a very hard winter that year. Drought stalked through the country like a vengeful corpse. The ground turned to iron and food was scarce as gold. Sickness spread, claiming many lives. When the bleak wind blew, it brought the pervasive stench of Death, feeding. The jakkals roved like ghouls amid the misery, caring nothing for the people's suffering, robbing them of what little they had. It made Zach very angry to hear the stories of their ruthlessness. But there was little he could do to stop them. He could not be Protector to all.

Still, he did what he could to assuage the great famine of need there. With the help of other teachers from the school, he set up soup kitchens and feeding schemes for the children. When the river dried up, he made our borehole water available to all who needed it. Desperate petitioners came streaming across the veld each day to our house. From first light you would find the patient queues forming; still there when I came back from school each afternoon. Jakkals came with them. But it was not thirst that was their reason.

'This borehole of yours; what an invaluable resource it is, in these thirsty times,' they purred in their underhanded way. 'It would be a tragedy for all in fact, if any harm should come to it – don't you agree? Pay us, and we will protect it for you. You can be sure no vandalism will happen here while we do the guarding.'

They were new to the pack, these particular jakkals. Young and vicious, but not altogether certain of their power yet. And this made them deadlier, for they felt the need to prove it. Zach however, was not in any mood to be diplomatic.

'Get off my ground, Maggots!' he said, with long-bottled anger. 'Your stink is not appreciated here. Take your threats somewhere else. Go – before I make you.'

'With what will you make us?' sneered the jakkals, their smiles full of rage as they stepped towards him.

Zach lifted his arm like a weapon, his fingers pointing the curse symbol at them. For he had learnt by now how to play on their superstitious fear of him. In the full blaze of the sunlight, the uncanny yellow of his hair was very prominent.

'Better for you if you do not ask,' he said, with soft assurance. 'For you will regret the answer, I promise you.'

The jakkals fell back at once. Their eyes were full of murder, but their fear of spells was greater than their rage. They twitched their blood-red talons at him, calling him an insulting name, which means Albino, in reference to his hair. They spewed threats at him – but from a prudent distance. Retreating, one of them ventured too close to the cogitating Cockroach, who promptly lashed out with an irritable hoof and caught the startled jakkal a square blow in the groin. He fell on his back, doubled-up and gasping – a very ignominious spectacle. The derisive laughter of the water-queues added insult to humiliation. I did not laugh with them. The humiliation of a jakkal is never cause for triumph. That I knew well.

I worried for days at the memory of that encounter – and its possible repercussions. I did not see how the jakkals could let things rest where they did. They had lost too much face in front of too many witnesses; for that they would blame Zach. They must now show their bite, find some way to erase that image of impotent ridiculousness they had presented; cause Zach to rue his scornful disregard of them. Or forever find their authority undermined.

Meanwhile, till they could get at him, they vented their pique on more compliant victims, harassing the poor burdened folk who came for our water, robbing them of their filled drums, which they then forced them to buy back for a very inflated fee. Zach was so enraged by their callous temerity that he couldn't sleep at night.
'Why do you allow them to abuse you this way?' he said to the people, on hearing their tales of persecution. 'Resist the bullies! Band together and fight back when they accost you. Stand up for yourselves.'

But nothing he said could rouse any spirit of rebellion in the people. They had lived too long under the tyranny of jakkals. The habits of submission, the conviction of their own weakness, was well ingrained in them. Endurance was the only defence they knew.

54

It was not long after this that Cockroach disappeared from our lives. I came home from school one afternoon to find her missing, inexplicably vanished into thin air. Naomi claimed not to have noticed her disappearance. The last she'd seen of the mule had been mid-morning, when she'd wrested one of Zach's shirts from her incorrigible old mouth and chased her from the house.

'She's probably off in the veld somewhere. Still sulking from the smack I gave her,' Naomi said, without too much concern. There was no sign of Cockroach in the veld, however. I searched for her for hours, calling her name till I was hoarse, my pockets loaded with tempting treats to lure her home again. But she was nowhere. I spread the word among the water-seekers that she had gone missing, asking them to be on the look-out for her. But some bleak knowledge told me that I wouldn't see her alive again.

Two days later, her severed head turned up on our doorstep, anonymously delivered; a gory and awful sight to me, her wide-open eyes fixed in the expression of reproachful surliness I knew so well. I wept inconsolably at the thought of the undignified death that must have come to her. I felt in some obscure way to blame, at fault for my lapsed vigilance, for allowing her to fall victim to human treachery once again. The world seemed very empty without her in it. I missed her irritable bray, her surly, snapping teeth, the rare and grudging moments of communion she allowed me. Of course I suspected jakkals. But they were not the only possible abductors. There was so much hunger that winter. Anything with flesh was food to hungry mouths. There was a good chance that my mule hadn't met her end at jakkal hands at all, but in some starving family's cooking pot. I don't know which possibility I abhorred more.

Then, in the midst of all the troubles of this bitter season, came news to overshadow all other concerns. Naomi was pregnant. The event astounded all of us, for we had long since come to accept her barrenness as a permanent condition. In spite of our differences, I was pleased for her. For I knew how much she had longed for this occurrence, how much secret pain the years of childlessness had caused her.

Zach could not contain his joy. Above all things, he longed to be a father. That cherishing instinct in him thrilled to the thought of some newborn helplessness, on which he might lavish all the tenderness that was in him. I watched, struggling with my envy, the new devotion in his manner towards Naomi, the private rapport of their glances, how the prospect of incipient parenthood seemed to bond them more closely than ever. I tried not to feel excluded by their mutual absorption, tried to rejoice for them, with them, to share in the mood of happy expectation that filled our hut.

It wasn't easy however. Naomi did not make it easy. With her pregnancy, she became even more guarded against me. Her hostility sizzled like an electric field. If I stood too close to her, she would start back, as though my nearness held contamination. She wouldn't allow me to touch her abdomen at all, no matter how I nagged and pleaded. That swelling belly of hers held great intrigue for me. It filled me with the same fascination that the ripening seeds of my garden once had. I was tantalized by the mystery of the hidden life inside it. It seemed to me like a giant, cryptic chrysalis. I longed to lay my hands on its fleshy outer casing, to feel the secret transformations happening within. My longings became so obsessive that I could think of nothing else.

One night, temptation overcame me. I crept up beside Naomi as she lay sleeping, carefully folded back her shift and pressed my hands to her enticing belly bulge. My palms thrilled to the smooth, firm feel of it. I felt the form of the babe inside it, curled like a brown seed in its ripeness, waiting for its time to be thrust out into the world. Its shape was male.

'Zach's son,' I thought. And yearning twisted like painful envy in my heart.

The babe turned fretfully under my fingers, as if sensing the intrusion of my thoughts.

'Sleep in peace, little brother,' I whispered to him. 'There is nothing for you to be afraid of. You are the son of a Shadow-slayer. And your sister is the girl who talks to cockroaches. Together we will guard your passage through this world of sorrows.'

Naomi woke. She cried out in fear and fury to find me crouched beside her with my hands covering her abdomen. She was sure I had put some disfiguring spell on the baby. And nothing Zach or I could say would quieten her hysterical ragings. Zach was very taken aback to hear the accusations that came flying from her lips against me. But to be fair, she did have reason for her mistrust.

She had caught me, the previous week, smearing the front door with my menstrual blood. It was for Zach's protection that I did it, a precaution against any treachery the jakkals might be planning. For I still waited with foreboding for their vindictiveness to manifest itself. Regularly, I dreamed of Zach's awful death at their hands.

Menstrual blood can be a useful ally to a woman sometimes. Its potency is greatly feared among the superstitious men of our parts. Even the most brutal will hesitate to rape a woman in her flow, believing it saps their virility. I was hoping that its repelling scent on our door would similarly safeguard us. When I tried to explain my reasons to Naomi, however, she would not listen. She scrubbed the offending substance off in fury, convinced my witchery had a darker motive; openly accusing me of devious designs on Zach.

The night she woke to find my hands on her belly only brought to a head what had been a long time in the brewing between us. The end result was that I was banished from the hut. I found this no real hardship, though. For the truth was, I was just as eager to quit that fraught and disturbing intimacy as Naomi was to be quit of me. Zach built me a room of my own – a tiny tin cell, hastily constructed out of whatever scraps he could get his hands on. And there I stayed for the rest of winter – isolated, but a little more content.

I say again; I did not blame Naomi for her treatment of me. In her shoes, I might have felt and acted just the same. Even at the height of the trouble between us, I understood this, and I bore her no grudges, no ill-will. I did not wish her any harm – the earth is my witness. I did not.

Ten

Winter ended. And the first spring month began. But there was no spring. Nothing budded, no new life stirred in the raddled wasteland that the veld had become. The white sun glared out of a desiccated sky, shrivelling – like an evil eye – whatever it alighted on. Dust and ashes were all the world was composed of. Storms brewed in far off places. But no rain fell, and the river remained empty. Even our borehole had dried up now, depleted by the excessive demands on it. We were forced to take our water from the school taps. Under cover of darkness, the Jungle people did the same. All night I heard the tramping of feet past our hut – saw in my dreams the ghostly sway of bodies with attenuated water-drum heads, gliding through the underworld tones of the veld.

Only the Jungle, in these desperate times, seemed to thrive. While its denizens thirsted and starved, it grew fatter. New influxes of refugees arrived daily to swell its population. Most of them were from the dustbowl rural areas. Driven by starvation to the urban fringes, in hope of finding a better chance of survival there. Shacks multiplied hectically, surging forward in wave upon wave, like a grey devouring tide. I watched the advance with an anxious, inward quivering. It seemed to me that the Jungle stalked us. One day, too late I feared, we'd wake to find its corrugated jowls pressed up against our throats.

The Newcomers were not welcomed by the Jungle's more established inhabitants. For their arrival only made scarcities scarcer. Clashes were frequent and the mood of the streets was ugly and tense. The jakkals exploited the friction with their usual shrewdness, siding with the Newcomers in their disputes with the other residents, wooing their loyalty with well-calculated strategy. They assisted them with materials for their shacks, for instance, selling to them at bargain prices what they had stolen from others. And the Newcomers asked no questions. Desperation does not fuss about its bedfellows. They were grateful only to have such powerful friends on their side.

I myself did not take too much to the strangers. I did not like the mood of sullen desperation they brought with them. I did not like the way they looked at me when I passed by, their critical eyes measuring my clothes, my nourished face, resentful of a wealth they did not have. In general, we had little to do with them, for they kept mainly to their own areas. But sometimes we encountered them, bartering for food with the Jungle traders, scrounging through the rubbish piles in search of anything they might use or hawk. Once, losing our way amid the shifting maze of lanes and byways, we strayed unintentionally into their quarters. It felt as if we had crossed over some invisible border, as if we trespassed where we had no right to be. Even Zach was disconcerted by the stone-faced inhospitality we encountered there. We both breathed more easily when we had found our way back to more familiar lanes again.

It was not difficult to lose your way these days, in the troubled and unstable chaos of that Jondolo city; even for those who knew it well, as we did. There seemed no permanence to anything. Routes were constantly changing, old lanes blocked off, new ones opening up. Shacks rose, shacks fell. Sometimes, an entire row of dwellings would unexpectedly vanish – overnight it seemed, leaving behind them an unnerving gap, like pulled teeth. It was the jakkals who were at the bottom of this mystery. They were greedy for materials, you see, to sell in the Newcomer quarters. So they put the fear of death into the shack occupants, harassing them mercilessly until they fled their homes, which they then dismantled at their leisure.

They did what they liked, those jakkals. Nobody tried to stop them. Nobody dared. Jungle survival teaches you to turn your head. Predators will feed when they will feed. Better to close your ears to your neighbour's wails and not interfere – lest you become the prey instead.

The sister of my former Jondolo neighbour was one of those on whom this misfortune fell. She was a good, outspoken woman, with a brave spirit of resistance in her, who had more than once offended jakkals with her defiant attitudes. Which was why they had earmarked her for this particular misery, I suspect.

Zach and I came upon her one day, standing in the bare plot where her shack used to be, keening her outraged anguish to the sky. While her bewildered infants clutched her skirts and sobbed with her.

'They have taken my home! They have taken all my things! Everything we had!' she wailed despairingly to the sympathetic crowd that pressed around her. 'What are we to do now? How will we live? They have left us with nothing!'

'Those vermin!' Zach swore, his face full of grief for her grief. 'Curse their stinking souls! I would like to burn the lot of them. They are excrement! Burning is what filth like that deserves!'

He was sallow with impotent rage, his eyes full of sulphur lightning. The injustice of this woman's plight aroused his Shadow-slayer's ire like nothing else.

'They must not be allowed to get away with this,' he said. 'When did it happen? How long ago were they here?'

'Last night,' one of the crowd ventured. 'We heard them. Their noise woke us. But we were too scared to go out and see what they were doing.'

'They took her things away at dawn this morning. In a cart,' a young boy said. 'I followed them to see where they went. They took it to sell among the amaGundane.'

AmaGundane was the name the people had given the Newcomers. It means the Rats.

'Could you show me?' Zach asked the boy. 'Do you remember the way they went?'

He said he did, and set off with confidence down one of the alley-paths, with Zach grimly striding behind him. The woman left her children in the care of one of the crowd and hurried, still weeping, after them. I followed much more reluctantly. My insides were churning with an uneasy premonition. I felt here some ill-starred chain of events being set into motion. Yet I could see no way to stop it. We followed our guide's brisk lead through the crooked network of lanes, towards the area of Newcomer shacks. My foreboding deepened as we stepped between the unfamiliar rows. I did not like the excrement smell of the air here, the way the shack sides pressed so closely upon us, like bodies, threatening. Faces watched us from the doorways. I was amazed at the hostility I saw in them. We did not know these faces. Yet it was as if we were known to them. Their looks said we had done some injury to them. Zach's greeting elicited no response but scowls. Mutterings grew behind us. A woman spat. Another made the sign of warding off evil. Evidently, it was Zach's hair that bothered them. Yet – there was more than mere superstition behind their surly antipathy. And whatever that more was, it frightened me.

I had a sudden crushing sense of treachery. The air up ahead seemed to be vibrating strangely to my eyes. The oppressing sense of shadows permeated every pore. I groped blindly for Zach's arm – to stop him, to pull him back from whatever perilous ambush it was that I sensed reaching for us. But our guide forestalled me. Halting suddenly, he jabbed his finger to point at something up ahead.

'There!' he said in triumph.

We stood beside a half-constructed row of shacks. Not far in front of us, a small crowd of people was gathering, milling round a handcart piled high with an assorted rubble of things. Grief wailed from the woman's throat as she caught sight of it.

'My things!' she cried. 'Those are my things they're selling – from my house. Stop them, stop them!'

Weeping, she ran to the rescue. Jakkals blocked her way. They looked beyond her and saw us, following. Loathing flew from their eyes. They were the same jakkals who had found such a humiliating reception at our borehole that day.

'Well, look!' they said with sneers. 'Look who comes here. It's our Albino friend. It's the Albino wizard and his ugly witch-whore.'

The crowd turned from their doings round the cart to stare our way. At the sight of Zach, a kind of growl went up. I saw faces hardening with the same inexplicable hatred that I'd noticed before.

'What do you want here, Wizard?' the jakkals mocked. 'Come to trouble these people with your dirty witchcraft? Are you looking for more human organs to buy? Or a few more babies to butcher, maybe, for your disgusting spells?'

I felt Zach's arm muscles jump under my hand. But he controlled himself, ignoring the jakkals to address himself to the Newcomers instead.

'I would not buy anything from these thieves, friends, if I were you,' he said. 'It will only bring you bad luck. The things on that cart are not theirs to sell. They belong to this woman here. These vermin stole them from her.'

'Oh, is that what she says,' the jakkals mocked. 'But this woman is a well-known liar. How can one believe anything she says! Besides, it is easy to accuse; one sheet of tin looks much like the next. If she claims these things are hers, then let her prove it.'

'But I can prove it!' cried the neighbour's sister, running to the cart in triumph. 'My materials are all marked with white dots of paint. My husband did that when we were building our shack, so that we could keep track of what was ours. See – here is white paint on this sheet! And this one – and this plank too . . .' She dodged around the cart, rummaging and exclaiming. A keening cry broke from her as she recognized other things.

'My cooking pot – here is my cooking pot! And look, these are my blankets . . . and my mugs! Everything on this cart is mine!' she trembled indignantly. 'Oh you thieves! How could you do this!'

Roughly, a jakkal hauled her down, knocking her sideways with a blow that sent her sprawling.

'Leave her!' Zach said, starting forward in fury. 'Touch her again, and I'll break your hand!'

'Oh, do you threaten me, Albino?' the jakkal said, very softly. There was no fear at all in his face, only a smirking kind of confidence. I looked into the black pits of his eyes and all courage failed me. For I saw our death there.

'Zach – ' I whispered urgently. 'Zach, come away – we must get away from here. Quickly Zach – while we can.'

But he was too angry to heed me. 'Give the woman back her things, Maggot,' he said. The jakkal laughed insultingly. 'Oh you wizards!' he said, pitching his voice deliberately for the crowd to hear. 'You think you own the world! You think because the people fear your power that you can threaten us and bully us and make our lives a misery as you please. But not all the people are such cowards as you believe. Their anger can be just as dangerous as your spells.'

As he spoke he addressed himself also behind us. Swinging round, I saw with a sinking heart that a second press of people had collected there. I recognized among them the same surly faces we'd passed on our way here.

'This is the Albino wizard – the one we have warned you about,' the jakkal told them. 'See his hair? This is the one you must thank for your many misfortunes. It is he that has called down this pestilent drought on our land. Who has stirred up the wrath of Ancestors against us with his awful spells.'

The Newcomers stood silent, listening or sceptical, it was impossible to judge. I felt their hatred for us, soaking the air like fuming petrol, needing just one spark to set it alight.

Too well I understood now the reason for the jakkals' gloating confidence. They had prepared well for this moment. They had found the way to have their revenge on Zach without any risk to themselves. The crowd was to be their instrument.

'Should he continue to walk free now, this Misery-Bringer?' the goading voice spoke on. 'Surely he deserves to pay for the great suffering he's caused you? Think of your wasted lands that you had to leave on account of him. Think of your cattle with their swollen tongues, lying too weak to rise. Think of your dead children.'

The crowd rumbled uneasily, a dull grief glowing in their eyes. They can be eloquent when they want to be, these jakkals. They always know how to press the nerve.

'The death of this arrogant Wizard would surely pacify our Ancestors,' a second jakkal voice suggested.

'Think what strong medicine we could make from his body parts!' shouted a third.

'Yes – kill him, kill him,' someone in the crowd chanted softly. Others took up the chant. And suddenly, it was a roar, a terrifying bellow, exploding simultaneously from dozens of angry throats. Zach tried to say something. But his voice couldn't be heard. I saw the neighbour's sister duck away in terror to hide herself under the cart. The boy who'd guided us was nowhere to be seen. A stone flew suddenly. Zach staggered back. When he took his hand away, I saw blood on his brow. The sight of his injury seemed to embolden the crowd. His blood was proof that he was not invincible; they thirsted for more. The chant changed its tenor.

'Stone him! Stone him! Let's tenderize the pig!' the voices shouted now. A few more missiles rained. But stones were scarce here.

'Why don't we rather cut the pig's throat? Then we can collect his blood for our muthi*!' a jakkal suggested.

The crowd liked that idea. An approving moan went up from them – almost a sexual sound. Their eyes had the avid blankness I had seen in killing mobs before; all logic, all humanity disengaged from their consciousness, infused with the liberating power of their mob strength.

It did not signify whether or not they believed the jakkals, whether they thought Zach really was to blame for their misfortunes. What mattered was that he was there – a convenient focus for their seethings. The dark gods of grief and despair stood at their shoulders, clamouring for sacrifice. Chance had delivered this scapegoat to them: any scapegoat would have done as well.

Still – though they craved to see his blood spilt, though they bayed for the 'evil wizard's' death, no-one yet had obeyed the jakkals' call to 'Seize him! Seize him!' I understood the thought that made them hesitate. And I made haste to play upon it.

'Yes – seize him – kill him – why do you hesitate?' I shouted, my voice shrill as a banshee's in my terror. 'Let's see who has the stupidity to lay hands on this powerful wizard. What man or woman is brave enough to risk the torments that his death will unleash? You will be cursed with terrible curses – rely on that! You will suffer madness! Fire will consume your entrails. Your organs will rot inside you. Your families will . . .'

* Muthi = medicine

My words were abruptly terminated. Rough arms seized me from behind. I saw something flash, felt a lip of steel press against my windpipe.

'So maybe we must cut your throat instead then, Witch,' a jackal's hot breath purred into my ear. 'What do you say, Albino? Should we kill your whore? We will cut her to pieces before your eyes – slowly, slowly . . .' The steel mouth caressed me; my face, my throat, my chest, leaving burning wetness where it touched.

'Let her go,' Zach said, his lips hardly moving. 'She is a child – only a child. Your quarrel is not with her.' His face was stone. But the smell of his fear was very evident.

'This is not the body of a child. This is a woman. And inside her is ancient evil,' the jackal said, gloating over Zach's helpless pallor. 'Is this face the face of a child?' he appealed for confirmation to the crowd.

'No!' they roared back obligingly.

'What should we do with this evil?'

'Burn it! Burn it!' the unhesitating response came.

'Roast the meat! Roast the meat! Roast the meat!'

The insistent monotone chant swelled like impassive thunder. There were men, women and children in that crowd. All of them calling for my death. The fixity of their faces terrified me. I saw the ecstasy of flame dancing in their eyes. I knew that they were far beyond the reach of reason now. Nothing would deflect them from the ritual of my death.

Remotely – for I was faint with horror – I heard a voice shout; 'Bring the tyre!'

The arm that gripped me jerked suddenly tighter. 'Stay back Albino!' the jakkal's voice grated behind me. 'Come no closer!'

'Zach!' I croaked. 'Run Zach – get away – save yourself!' I struggled to see him through the mist of my terror.

'Stay back I said – Wizard, stay back . . .'

I was thrust violently aside. The jakkal's hand delved for the pocket of his coat. There was a loud concussion. Zach staggered, sagged. I heard a scream that cleaved the universe apart – and realized it was mine.

'Zach, Zach!' I whimpered trying to run to him. But every cell felt paralysed. I watched, faint and nauseous, as he fought to keep himself from falling. His hand was pressed against his breast. His face had the colour of death in it. I waited for blood to blossom through his fingers, for the life-blood of his heart to come pumping out into his hand. A single droplet oozed; not red, but brassy-gold, this droplet; bullet-gold. It rolled down his shirt-front, dropped to the ground and lay there like an omen in the dust.

Amazement held me spellbound. Beside me, the jakkals stood equally transfixed. A great hush washed over the crowd. It seemed for an instant as though all sound had been sucked from the world. I was the first to recover. Darting forward, I snatched up the bullet, displayed it aloft for all to see.

'See the power of this wizard!' I croaked through

71

my clogged throat. 'Even bullets cannot harm him. Even Death is afraid to touch him. See how the bullets run like water off his skin!' I grabbed Zach's arm and pulled him with me like a sleepwalker towards the thick of the crowd.

'Let us through! Let the wizard through!' I hissed at the nervous faces. 'Back – back – take care his hand does not brush against you! For it has a pestilent touch. Take care your look does not anger him, Sister. Or he may curse you with the terrible affliction of the wasting disease . . .'

In this way, I forced our passage through the mob. They parted before us like tall grass. No-one made any attempt to block us. Not one dared to lift a hand against us. The display of Zach's invincibility against bullets had sobered and disquieted them. Whatever the powerful medicine was that he had access to, they concluded it was better not trifled with.

Even so, I could not believe that we were to be allowed to escape with our lives after everything. I was sure that the jakkals at least, would not be so easily cheated of their victims. As we fled back along the unfamiliar alleyways, I kept imagining I heard the mob baying behind us. My skin constantly quivered in anticipation of assailing missiles. Every figure in a doorway was a source of ambush to my eyes.

Finally, however, we found ourselves in safer territory. We stopped, embracing exhaustedly. For a long time we could not speak, only cling to each other, our bodies trembling together like agitated water.

'Look how they cut you,' Zach whispered, his hand very gentle as it traced the stinging wounds on my face and breast.

'It's nothing,' I croaked. I buried my head in the warm, vital flesh of his neck, overwhelmed by the enormity of the miracle that had kept him alive.

'How is it you aren't dead?' I whispered tremulously. 'They shot you, Zach! I saw the bullet hit you! It isn't possible that you weren't harmed!'

'It's because of you,' he said very softly. He turned his head and rubbed his cheek with fervour against my own. 'It was this that saved me. Your talisman. Look!'

He put his hand into his shirt and lifted out the Toad Tree amulet to show me. A small hole gaped like a startled mouth in the wrinkled flesh of the old pod.

'This is what the bullet hit. If I hadn't been wearing it, I wouldn't be alive now.' He shook his head, smiled a grey, exhausted smile into my eyes. 'When you gave this to me all those years ago, you said there was magic in it. I believe you now!'

Eleven

We crawled home, reaching our hut as dusk was falling. A sullen sunset smouldered. A great unresolved tension charged the air. I felt pursued still. Hostility was all around us, leaking from the fraught sky, from the Jungle behind us. I felt that our escape from trauma was only a temporary reprieve.

Zach thought it best that Naomi should not be told of our ordeal, for her time was near now, and he was anxious to spare her unnecessary upset. We explained away my cut face, Zach's bruised brow, on a scuffle with would-be thieves. But Naomi sensed, I think, that there was more to the story; for she was no fool. And though we tried to keep up the pretence of normality, our strain showed through. Our pallid faces and troubled silences must have been evidence enough to her that something graver was amiss. Yet she asked no questions, perhaps fearing the replies.

That night, alone in my small room, I found it impossible to sleep. For in sleep, dreams lurked. And those, I had no courage to face. Every time I closed my eyes, I saw the crowd, with their blank, avid faces, baying for my death. My skin still tingled from the voltage of their hatred. I smelled its acrid smell, permeating my pores like smoke. Hatred sought us still – of that I was certain. I felt its unfocused rage in the air of the night, seeking the catharsis of which it had been cheated.

In this, I was wrong, though I didn't know that then. Catharsis had in fact been found. The neighbour's sister had been discovered by the mob after we left, in her hiding place under the cart. Jakkals had dragged her out. They doused her with paraffin and set her alight, while the crowd danced their vengeance dance around her burning body. To this day, her death still haunts me. For I know it was a substitute for ours.

I must have slept eventually. For I jerked awake towards midnight, hearing the pelt of missiles striking the tin roof of my room. 'So it has come then,' I thought in my sleep-befuddled terror. Through the narrow window came a searing flash, the crack of some more drastic weaponry. Then the gush and roar of descending water, pouring from the sky. It took a while for it to dawn on me that it was rain that I was hearing. Rain!

I opened the door of my room and let its freshness wash in on the wind. The scent of wet dust, and fragrant grass filled my nostrils. The din on my roof was deafening, exhilarating! Drowning out all thought, all fear. I shed my clothes and danced into the storm like a dervish. Lightning flashed and thunder roared and the darkness poured around me like the world dissolving. Cold, scourging drops lashed my skin. I felt all the desperate ugly terror of the day turn light and fluid inside me, floating out like scummy effluent on the waters of the storm. I looked around. And there was another figure dancing with me. He was naked too, his body a brown tree, streaming water from every limb. We did not say a word to each other. The storm spoke for us. In the wild abandon of the night, all bottled feeling found expression. Zach's hand strayed out to clench mine tightly. And we stood side by side, submissive yet exultant, waiting for the sky to expend its passion.

Twelve

We were coming back from school together, trudging up the last long hill that led to our hut; not speaking much, for we were both given to our silences these days, our minds weighted with thoughts too troubled to share. The day had the bright, soft look of newly-washed things. Three days of solid rain had swept all trace of drought away. The river was flowing strongly again. There were flowers in the veld, there was green stubble sprouting from the tired old grasses, a feeling of spring innocence to everything. Yet I could not bring myself to trust in it. I felt perpetually on edge – unsettled as I had been ever since the day of our ordeal with the mob. I could not seem to leave the experience behind me. I could not shake off the sense of dread it had engendered in me, the conviction that we were not to be allowed to escape so unscathed from the confrontation; that there were reverberations still to be felt.

We twisted up the final curve of the hill, skirting the muddy dam that had formed at its apex. I looked across the strip of veld towards our hut.

And saw for a moment, its facade all twisted, screams reflected in its windowed eyes. A terrible sick foreboding slammed me. I could not take another step.

'Zach – ' I said in terror, 'Zach!'

He looked at me, surprised. Concerned.

'What's wrong!' he said. 'What is it Marinda? What's the matter?'

But I could only shake my head and say again; 'Zach – oh Zach!'

'Tell me!' he said, my dread infecting him. 'Speak Marinda!' For pity's sake say what's wrong!'

'The house . . .' My teeth were chattering so much I could hardly get the words out. 'Naomi . . . don't go in there, Zach,' I wept, 'Oh don't – don't!'

I saw his eyes expand with trepidation. Books tumbled unheeded from his arms as he sprang forward, calling Naomi's name. I raced alongside, crying 'Be careful! Be Careful! Zach!' But he paid no heed.

The first thing I saw when we reached the hut was the unearthed skull of the rat I'd buried in my childish naivety those many years ago. Its empty sockets mocked me. Its grinning malice warned me to expect a gruesome find. An old, familiar stink assailed my shrinking nostrils; that unmistakable Jondolo smell of shadows and corpses.

I heard Zach's choked cry of anguish beside me. I raised my reluctant eyes to the door, where he was staring. Something was nailed there; a blood-drenched bundle, tied up in a sacking sling. The sight of it set up seismic tremblings inside me. I did not need Zach's groans to know what terrible trophy it contained; a little ripe grub, black-haired and silky-skinned. A plump and precious seed on the verge of its unfurling, wrenched out of its womb-bed and delivered into death instead. I felt my insides heave in outrage, fought down with difficulty the spew that rose from my guts. There was more abomination waiting.

In a room full of blood, Naomi lay. A broken doll inelegantly sprawled. Her desecrated womb gaped like a bloody abyss. There were other atrocities too; but I shall not name them. Her locked grimace of agony will haunt me forever, I think. The brutal manner of her death bore the unmistakable jakkal signature.

They are not men like other men, these jakkals. They have no humanity in them. I have lived under the shadow of their ruthlessness for most of my life. Yet I still do not understand what fabric they are made of. Is it genes that determine their particular depravity? Or is it merely life in this Jungle hell that has warped them? Suckled on its cruelties, denied all other sustenance, they fill themselves on hate, since hate is all they know. Yet what does it help to understand these things? It does not make their inhumanity any easier to bear.

Zach's grief was terrible. Its violence frightened me. He was deaf, blind to all my clumsy attempts at consolation. I could bring him no solace, no matter how I tried. That is the special skill of jakkals; they know how to wield the blow that cripples most. It was not just the loss of Naomi and his son that so grieved him. It was the awfulness of the death that had been inflicted on them. He knew well enough that he was the reason for their exaggerated suffering. And the knowledge was very bitter.

For a time, he was a little crazed, I think. He ranted through the Jungle with his face wild as a prophet's, threatening death to all jakkals, demanding the culprits surrender themselves into his hands. The jakkals let him rant. They laughed at his wild grief, turned their backs contemptuously on his raging accusations and went on with their conversations as though he wasn't there. They taunted him deliberately with their smirking indifference. And when in his frustration, he was driven to lash out at them, they made a sport of his mad rage, goading him from all sides till he did not know which way to swing, shadowboxing with him as one might with a child – or an imbecile; sending him tripping ignominiously into the garbage to lie there, vanquished by his own humiliation.

They did not need to lay a hand on him to achieve their purpose. It suited them to have him display his impotence in this public way. They could not have made their point more tellingly if they had put a rope around his neck and paraded him, naked through the alleys.

'See this powerful wizard!' their sneering faces said. 'This wizard that even bullets cannot strike! What good are his spells and potions to him now! Beware then of arousing the wrath of jakkals. Lest you too suffer the bite of their displeasure.'

Weeks passed. And they were very black days in our house. The hut stank so of despoilment that we could hardly bear to breathe its air. The blood marks would not come off the door. Though I scrubbed and scrubbed, I could not scrub the bloody stigma away. There was no sanctuary to be found in that hut now. Only grim reminders of the outrage that had happened there. Zach was as unnerved by the place as I was. He slept at night in my small room with me, his long body stretched out in the cramped space beside me, his spirit barely present. The burden of his mourning still oppressed him as heavily as ever. He was strange and withdrawn from me, taking interest in nothing. Going through the motions of daily living without conviction.

I could not bear to see my Shadow-slayer so transformed. I understood too well his trouble. But I had no remedy. It was not grief alone that galled him, but the need for vengeance. Naomi's corpse sang in his ear in the way of all corpses, berating him for his impotence, demanding that her sufferings be paid for. It was a torment to him to have to sit helpless, knowing that her slaughterers went free. The first lesson of obeisance is always the most bitter to swallow: to accept the unacceptable, meekly to bow the head to injustice when everything in you cries out for protest and revolt. Impotence cripples the will like nothing else.

Slowly, painfully, we tried to reconstruct the trembling fragments of our lives. But the jakkals were not finished with us yet. They had only crippled the rebel, not destroyed him. More suffering was required.

A pack of them waylaid us in the Jungle one day, blocking the narrow way in front of us so that we had no choice but to stop. Their spokesman was our old enemy from the borehole encounter.

'You must go from this vicinity, Wizard,' he said, his voice chilling us with its softness. 'We are tired of seeing your Albino face in our streets. You are not welcome in these precincts anymore. Find yourself another place to live.'

'Move out of my way, Maggot-scum,' Zach ground out through unmoving lips. 'Before I knock you down.'

There was a trembling in his face that wasn't fear. I saw the way his fists bunched themselves reflexively, and grabbed onto his arm in haste.

'You are not listening my friend,' the jakkal said. He put his face very close to Zach's. They might have been lovers, these two, were it not for the death-duel of their eyes. 'We are telling you that you must go. Better to listen while we say it politely.'

'Your trouble-making has been tolerated long enough here,' spoke up a second jakkal loudly.

'A wizard has no business teaching in our schools,' a third said. 'Corrupting our children. Practising your black arts on their innocence.'

'I have never done that and you know it,' Zach said, his eyes glittering like bullet-brass in a face of yellow-grey.

'Take our advice,' the first jakkal said. His voice was a knife encased in velvet. 'Leave while it is still easy. You have had your share of adversity already. Why court more?'

'You think I will be chased out of my home because you say so?'

'If you are wise, you will go before you are chased. You will not like our methods of persuasion. That I promise you.'

'You have already done your worst. What more have I to fear from you?' Zach said, very bleakly.

'Don't tempt us to show you!' the jakkal snarled.

'Don't threaten me! Or this Wizard may be forced to make threats of his own!'

'No threats. Only a little good advice,' the jakkal sneered.

'*This* for your advice then!' said Zach in rage. He lashed out forcefully with his fist. The jakkal fell back against his fellows, blood gushing from one nostril. His hand flashed to the pocket of his coat, apparently thought better of the impulse, slowly withdrew.

'Oh Albino – you will rue this. I will make you rue this,' he said, stemming the bloody nasal tide with his fingers. His murderous eyes slid for one jolting moment to my face. Then he turned on his heel and strode away, his fellows with him. Zach and I stood where they'd left us, shaken and silent.

'We will have to do as they say. We will have to go away,' I said through fearful lips.

'I am going nowhere. I will not be chased out of my home by scum and offal,' Zach answered woodenly.

'They will not rest until they have made you. You will go in the end,' I said.

'How will they make me?' He smiled, a graveyard smile that highlighted the sallow gauntness of his face. 'What more can they take from me than they have already taken?'

'Your life!' I whispered, tears of dread coursing down my cheeks.

'No, that they will not dare.' He slung a reassuring arm around my shoulders, grimaced again his painful travesty of a smile. 'I am the invincible wizard, remember? The one that bullets cannot harm. They will not risk striking at me directly. They are too cowardly for that.'

A sudden thought crossed his face. 'But you . . .' he faltered, gripping me to him fearfully.

'I am your witch-whore,' I reminded him, trying to make light of it. 'They would not dare to touch me either.'

We went on with our lives. But it was not easy. Every day required an act of courage to get through. We felt watched, stalked. We felt the burning trajectory of jakkal thoughts seeking us out wherever we went. Every trip into the Jungle seemed like a venture into the jaws of ambush. Zach refused to stay away.

'We have friends there,' he insisted stubbornly. 'They need us. How can we just abandon them? I will not have my actions dictated to by gangster scum!'

But the war of nerves wore even his resistance down. It was the waiting that was the hardest. We knew the blows would come. But in what form, we couldn't anticipate. Petty disasters began to plague us. Our borehole pump was sabotaged. Thieves broke into our hut one day and stole half our possessions. One night, I woke to find a jakkal standing like death's shadow at my elbow. But when I cried out, he evaporated into darkness and smoke.

The principal of Zach's school called him in one day. Jakkals had been to visit him.

'You have a sorcerer on your staff,' they said. 'The one with the albino hair. Get rid of him.'

The principal refused. For he was a fair man, and he knew Zach's worth too well to be influenced by trouble-makers. But he was fearful all the same. For he understood very well the threat implied in the words of his visitors.

The next day, when he went to his car after school, he found the tyres slashed to ribbons and the windscreen smashed with bricks. The day after that, his dog was poisoned. He called Zach in again.

'I have the safety of the children to consider,' he said. 'You are a good teacher, Zach. You will easily find another position elsewhere.'

'I want no other position,' Zach said.

'We will be very sorry to see you go, of course. You have been an invaluable asset to this school. Everyone will miss you.'

'I am not going,' Zach said immovably.

'You are not making this very easy, Zach,' the principal reproached him. 'Do you not understand that I don't do this thing from choice? We have seen already what those hoodlums are capable of.

If I don't give in to them now, who knows what they may resort to.'

'Let them do whatever they will do,' Zach replied harshly. 'But I am staying.'
'It is not up to you!' said the principal, growing angry in his agitation. 'You are dismissed, I said. And that is the end of it. Pack your things and be gone from here by the end of the week. Substitutes will be appointed to your classes.'

'Is this my thanks then, for eight years of service?' Zach accused him. 'To be dismissed, on the whim of gangsters, for no fault of my own?'

'The safety of the pupils is my paramount consideration,' said the principal uncomfortably.

'Your own, you mean,' Zach said. 'It's cowards like you that those gangsters draw strength from.'

I have already said that he was not himself during that time. It was not his usual way to expect others to put themselves in jeopardy on his behalf. But this new dark fever of obstinancy that possessed him had made him hard and indifferent to all dilemmas but his own. His personal war with the jakkals obsessed him to the exclusion of everything. He had lost too much to them to capitulate now – whatever the cost.

Thirteen

That same night, deep in the small hours, I was woken from a troubled sleep by some presentiment – some frightening, lucid dream of burning and flames. Shadows shuddered on the walls of my eyelids. For a second, the impression of conflagration was so strong, I thought it was our hut that was burning. I leapt up urgently to shake Zach awake.

'Zach – fire – there's fire – it's the school – the school's burning, Zach!' I cried.

He didn't ask me how I knew, but raced outside with me at once, barefoot and shirtless. We stood at the top of our hill, looking down in dismay at the smouldering view below us. Flames twitched with vivid energy in the dark wasteland beside the factories. A shuddering red dragon reared and lashed itself against the sky. The sound of its roaring reached us distantly. The air was bitter with its smoky breath.

'Curse them! Oh, those devils!' Zach cried, passing his hand across his eyes. He started forward despairingly, stumbling blindly down the dark hillside, with me beside him. Though we knew, even as we ran, that our haste was in vain. The clapboard walls of the school would offer scant resistance to the flames. By the time we reached it, there would be little left to save.

It was not easy to find our way there, though we knew it so well. The dark night was made even darker by the smoky pall in the air. A hot wind flew up the hill to sear our faces. Soot rained like crumbling moth wings into our eyes.

Panting and exhausted, we reached the burning ruins at last. An eerie desertion gripped the scene. The rest of the world was deeply asleep at this hour, apparently oblivious to the disaster on its doorstep. No figures other than our own were in sight. The stink of jakkal treachery was unmistakable, however. The school writhed painfully in its death-throes, showering burning wreckage into the wind.

'My books! All my books are in there!' I heard Zach cry. He darted forward. But the hot breath of the dragon beat him back. The sound of its feeding was like the beating of giant vulture wings. Inside the vibrating heart of the furnace, I could see the charred wreckage of desks, gnawed and dismembered. Flame gushed up in a sudden tidal wave as some resinous thing was ignited. The last standing wall collapsed. Zach's face jerked and twisted in the distorting light as if he too was being consumed.

'There's nothing left!' he said with hollow anguish. 'It's all destroyed – everything's destroyed.' And in a bitter undertone: 'They have left me with nothing.'

'You have me!' I told him timidly, echoing the words he'd said to me once, long ago, in my bereavement. 'We still have each other, Zach.'

He turned his head to me, his eyes full of the shuddering of shadows. 'Yes, it's true. I still have my little sister,' he said with pain.

He embraced me and we hugged each other fiercely, our bodies vibrating with a kindred agitation. I could feel the beat of Zach's heart, strong and rapid against me, the heat and smoothness of his naked skin.

I felt the hopeless gush of my love for him, drenching my heart in its bleak, sweet pain.

'Don't leave me Zach – oh don't leave me ever!' I whispered, out of my great fear of losing him. He did not answer, only hugged me closer, burying his head against my neck. There was a rough urgency in the way his arms held me. I sensed in him some pent-up storm that both frightened and elated me; a longing for abandon that matched my own.

'We have only each other now,' his unsteady whisper said into my ear.

He lifted his head and passed his trembling hands over my head, my face. His own face was very close to mine. We stood tensely, breathing each other's breath. Then he touched his mouth to mine.

It was a lover's kiss, not the kiss of a brother for his sister. I felt its heat in every pore. I felt its sweetness and its fire devouring me. When Zach drew his head back to look at me, I saw the burning of the dragon in his eyes.

'Marinda!' he said, breathing the word harshly, like a sound of pain.

'Oh, Marinda my sister. My love.'

He kissed me again, more deeply, urgently. Inside my body, a strange, wild dance began. It thrummed and pulsed to the touch of his hands the way it did when it was under the violin's spell. As if my body was the violin.

I stroked my palms over his naked back, his chest, revering the lean strength of his body, its vital textures. A red larva-light of flame flowed over the brown landscape of his skin. I stripped my shift off impatiently, wanting to join my burning to his, wanting no encumbrances between his flesh and mine.

'I have wanted this!' I told him breathlessly, pressing my nakedness to him without shame. 'Oh, how I have longed for this, Zach! For so long. So long.'

My words, or my action, seemed to jolt him. A troubled look crossed his face. Dismay cooled the yellow passion of his eyes.

'But this is wrong,' he muttered, guiltily drawing his body away from mine. 'What am I doing? Oh, Marinda – what am I thinking of! You're my little sister – this is so wrong! So wrong.'

He stooped to retrieve my shift, made to put it over my head again. But I fought it impatiently.

'Why is it wrong?' I challenged him. 'What can be wrong about it? There is nothing unnatural in what we're doing. I'm not your sister, Zach. And I love you!'

I tried to press myself close to him again. But again, his hands warded me off.

'You're not ready for love! You're still a child – you're just a child!' he said remorsefully.

'I'm fifteen,' I reminded him impatiently. 'That's old enough to know what love is. I have known since I was eight. I have loved you since then – since the first day I ever saw you.'

'It was a child's love,' he said. 'It is a child's love still.'

His blind insistence frustrated me.

'Is this the body of a child?' I challenged him, grabbing his hand and pressing it to my breast. But he snatched it back as though the touch had blistered him.

'Don't – please Marinda,' he said with pain. 'You only make this harder – don't you understand? There can't be any sexual love between us! I have cared for you like a little sister. I have loved you for years like a brother, a protector – one who stands between you and the world's violations. You are as close to me as my own heart is. But I can't be your lover. There would be too much betrayal in that.'

He saw that I was about to argue further.

'No, please – just go. Leave me for a while,' he said. 'I need to think. Go back to the hut. I'll join you there. We'll talk more then.'

I did as he asked, though reluctantly. I left him there, my Shadow-slayer, to do his solitary brooding beside the smoking ruins of the school and I made my way back to the hut alone. In truth, I was not too dismayed by my dismissal. For I too needed private time for thought. A bewildering confusion of emotions filled me – frustration, elation, sorrow over the school's destruction, apprehension for our future. Laughter and tears were lodged inextricably together in my throat.

Yet deeper than all of it, was a great suffusing happiness. Love throbbed through my body, every cell alive with it, lit by its transforming flame. I could still feel the sweetness of Zach's kiss vibrating inside me, the imprint of his warm mouth on mine. I wanted to taste it again, to feel again his yearning body pressed to mine. The knowledge that he desired me just as much was all that helped to quieten my frustrated longing. For I knew that for all his disclaiming, what he felt for me was no chaste love. In time, I was sure I must be able to overcome his foolish scruples. In time, I would wear his resistance down.

I turned and looked back down the long slope of the hill, towards the black hulk of the school, still sullenly smouldering. Embers winked like savage stars through the heavy pall of smoke. I made out Zach's crouching shape in the fitful glow, the glimmer of his hair, barely perceived, like faint starlight.

'Your heart is mine!' I whispered to him fiercely over the distance. 'Our souls are one. Nothing but death can part us now.'

A cold catspaw of wind reached out of the night to touch my nape, raising gooseflesh of disquiet. I wanted superstitiously to bite the words back, to snatch them out of the ear of the wind, to have them unsaid. In front of me, dawn was breaking, blood against the black edge of the sky. I trudged on towards it, wondering at the sudden icy bleakness in my heart.

Fourteen

I waited half the morning for Zach to come back to the hut. I lay in my small room, drowsing and dreaming, my senses strained for sounds of his return. The room was filled with his scents, his imprints. I breathed them in with every breath; and every breath intensified my impatient longing. I ached for the moment of his return, for the sight of his tall figure outlined in the doorway. But the morning grew later and still he did not appear. Worry began to gnaw uneasily at my insides.

I rose and went outside to see if I could see any sign of him. The day was hot, oppressive, the air still acrid from the aftermath of fire. There was cruelty in the unrelenting blue of the sky. The Jungle leered mishapenly from its close distance, its iron roofs glinting like teeth in the sun. I shivered without reason. I did not like the feeling in this day. Something waited in it, something violent and inescapable.

I went back to the school, to see if I could find

Zach there. It made a depressing sight in the daylight with its blackened stumps of walls and ruined fragments. Teachers and children milled in bewilderment amid the sooty wreckage, scratching through the rubble to see what could be salvaged. The principal stood bitter-mouthed to one side, surveying his ruined fiefdom. He did not respond when I asked him if he'd seen Zach there. Only turned his back on me. Wherever I mentioned Zach's name, I drew the same sullen unresponsiveness. Rumour had spread that he was the catalyst for this disaster. It hurt to see how ready they were to make a pariah of him; he who had given so much of himself to these pupils, this school.

I went back to the still-deserted hut. But I couldn't stay there. I was too wound up with worry now, my heart knocking with a dread I couldn't quiet. I thought I knew the reason for Zach's prolonged absence. It was obvious to me that he'd gone into the Jungle, to seek confrontation with the jakkals over this latest outrage of theirs. All strength drained from me as I thought that thought. I saw him, armed with nothing but his foolish courage, facing down the treacherous pack in his usual impetuous way. This time, my deep foreboding told me, there would be no fortuitous escape for him. This time, the jakkals would not let the hated foe walk free. They might be too cowardly to lay hands on him themselves. But there were plenty they could coerce to do so in their stead. A single assassin planted in an alleyway, and the nuisance would be removed from their orbit for good. Bitterly I cursed myself for having left him, for not realizing his intentions sooner; for allowing myself to be distracted by my untimely daydreams.

I flew on wings of fear into the Jungle. Urgency impelled me through the alleys with scant regard for atmosphere. I could think of nothing but Zach and his danger. Of danger to myself, I had no thought at all. Prescience tried to warn me. But I wasn't paying enough attention to its voices. I felt the foreboding, but mistook its cause. I smelled the smell. But in my haste, I did not heed it. It never occurred to me that the disaster I sensed in this disquieting day might be coiled to strike at me.

They came at me from the dark mouth of a side alley. There were two of them; I do not know who they were. They were not jakkals. But I think it was at the behest of jakkals that they accosted me. For they called me the witch-whore. And it was clear from other things they said that their attack was long premeditated. They had the advantage of surprise as well as strength. Before I knew it, I was crushed between them, their iron embrace forbidding struggling, much less escape. They dragged me into the alleyway and forced me down on a bed of filth and garbage. I smelt the liquor on their breath. Saw chemical madness in their eyes. Their eyes were bright and pitiless as steel.

One held me down while the other invaded me. They took it in turns, breaking into my body with great brutality. I tried not to scream as their organs ripped me and tore me. For I knew my screams would drive them to more gleeful frenzy. I tried to tell myself that it was only my body they were invading, only my flesh that they were abusing. But it felt like my soul itself was being violated. I couldn't retreat deep enough to escape the terror and pain.

The rape was not enough for them. My silence annoyed them I think. So they hit me till my screams burst out of me. They raped me again, nibbling at my bloodied face like greedy flies. When they had finished, they carved their names on my breasts with knives. Then doused me with their urine and left me in my naked shame for the flies to laugh at.

I could not move, I could not weep. I could only lie there, shaking and sick, my whole body burning like an open wound. My eyes were full of blood and urine. The excrement smell of myself made me sick to my bones. I lay there the whole day, hidden under garbage, terrified to let myself be seen in my state of shame, to exhibit myself to strangers' eyes. Also, I did not know where to go to. I couldn't go back to the hut. I couldn't bear to have Zach witness my defilement. I was afraid the image of this ugliness would be branded forever into his vision, that forever after when he looked at me, I'd see the stain of it reflected in his eyes.

When night came, I dragged myself up at last. Instinct impels the wounded animal towards the deepest bolt-hole, where it can hide and heal in safety and darkness. So I crawled back to my black hole – the odorous womb of the old Jondolo. It was still untenanted, barely habitable now, half-collapsed, full of damp and rot. But it suited my need all the better for that. The corpses welcomed me back with greedy embrace, calling my name in gleeful mockery; 'Sorrow! Sorrow!'

The rats chuckled their spite. I wept with gratitude to be among such unwholesome company. In the midst of this ugliness I felt less stained. At night, when the corpses howled for their vengeance, I screamed with them. I listened eagerly for the sounds of slaughter and burning. They filled me with savage exultance. I didn't care whose death, whose blood paid for my sufferings. I wanted scapegoats; any scapegoat would do.

Days passed. I have little recollection of them. I lived like a shadow among shadows. The world outside the shack had no reality for me. I think I was very sick for a time. A strange, hectic fever infested my body. The cuts on my breasts turned septic. My face was so swollen I could not eat. It was only because of the kindness of neighbours that I survived at all; one woman in particular. I am ashamed to say I did not ever learn her name. I hadn't known her before, and I have never seen her since. But it was she who took care of me, asking no questions. Cleaning me, feeding me, tending my injuries. I saw in her eyes the scars of her own befoulment. She knew what violation was.

Once, I thought that Zach came looking for me. Whether it was only a delirious dream or he was really there, was impossible to say. I opened my eyes and I saw his brightness flooding the doorway. So sharp. Like a blade of reproach. I shrank into my corner, in a terror of his eyes discovering me. He called my name; 'Marinda. Marinda.'

But the shadows answered him and said – there is only Sorrow here. And he went away and did not come again.

Fifteen

It is a curious thing, that when life tastes most bitter, the chord that binds us to the world is at its most enduring. In the black pit where I was imprisoned, existence had no value. I had no wish to keep on surviving. Life seemed to me a grotesque imposition, and I shrank from the prospect of continued subjugation to its horrors. Yet I could not die. My body breathed on. My mouth opened to take the food the neighbour brought. My blood-cells fought the infections. My torn flesh closed.

Slowly, slowly, healing came. The pit released its dark hold on my spirit; but now, a different sickness plagued me. I was beset by constant nausea, by violent, convulsive retching. My breasts throbbed with a strange tenderness. I felt with despair and loathing the secret swelling of my stomach. It was not hard to guess the cause. The knife-wounds on my breasts were not the only legacy my assaulters had left me. They had planted in me the seed of their evil. I felt it lodged inside me, in my deepest centre, swelling, swelling like a tick in my womb. The knowledge of it drove me to fresh frenzies of self-loathing. I wanted to tear my insides out to get at it. My body retched and retched, trying in vain to expel the hated parasite. I loathed it with every fibre of my being. Nothing but its death would appease my outrage. The dark gods demanded sacrifice. And this scapegoat would do.

I found a spike, filthy and rusty now, loosed from the old rat-trap that Zach had made. Its tip was stained with old rodent blood. But in my mind, it shone like an avenging sword. Gloatingly I pressed it to the bulge of my belly, imagining the satisfying moment of piercing – the tick punctured, shrivelling, its bloody corpse dropping down like faecal matter to be expelled. I knew full well that in causing its death, I might cause my own. But that mattered little to me then. If anything, I welcomed the prospect.

I lay down to prepare myself for the ritual of slaughter. I laid my hands on my belly, to feel the parasite's exact location. Deep inside the bulge, I sensed its alien presence – a tiny helplessness, floating fishlike in its sac of amniotic fluid. Snugly it rested there, so trusting; thinking itself safe in its secret womb chamber, protected from all the world's treachery. Yet here was the world, poised to invade even that sanctuary.

Tears gushed from my eyes in sudden floods. I flung the spike away from me, loathing myself for my weakness. Yet unable to commit the deliberate betrayal. The thought was too strong in my mind of that other womb invaded, that other infant life torn out, so brutally terminated before it could begin. Between that violation and the one I planned, what difference was there? And since I could see none, what choice did I have except to bear with my repugnance for this unwitting invader, until the time came to deliver it more naturally into the world.

There is little to report about the time that followed. I lived in a limbo of waiting, all my will, my every thought centred on the unwanted lodger in my womb; living for the day when I would be free of its galling presence at last. I observed with cold indifference the changing shape of its development. Felt, unimpressed, the ripples of its movement, the lusty kicking of its feet. I knew that it was male. But the knowledge brought me neither pleasure nor regret. I tolerated its presence in my body, that was all. There was no love or tenderness in me towards it. I had not invited it into me. And I cared little what happened to it once the time came for it to be expelled.

The rats and I had many conversations about its future. 'An unwanted child is a heavy burden in this life,' they told me. 'Why not leave it here with us? We will make quick work of the problem.'

'It is the offspring of excrement,' they reminded me. 'You owe it no allegiance. You will always see in it the reminder of your pain.'

The arguments were beguiling. I could see that what they said made sense.

The long-awaited day arrived at last. I did my own delivery, preferring no witnesses to what I was planning. My labour was violent and agonizing. The baby forced its way out of me with as much trauma as it had gone in. But my cries of pain were tempered with triumph. For it was a joy to know the parasite was being expelled at last.

It was close to dawn when he finally emerged from between my bloody thighs; a male child, as I had known it would be. I held him against me exhaustedly while I gathered strength for the next move. I had not expected him to be so small. Or his smallness to be so perfect. His breathless cries pierced me with remorseful pain. The rats clustered eagerly, their red eyes burning from the shadows.

'Deliver him up. Fulfil your promise. We are waiting.' But I could not. He was so defenceless, so unguarded. I saw his soul, wide open to the assaults of the world. And I wept for his innocence, for the harms that must come to him. He had been thrust into me unasked, with violence and brutality. But I saw now that he was as much a victim of that offence as I was. He had not asked to be created into this world of horrors. And what was to become of him now, I didn't know.

I put him to my breast and let him suckle. I felt his blind mouth seeking, nuzzling for the nipple. He found it, and sucked contentedly, in trust and comfort. My tears flowed faster. I stroked my hand over his silken infant skin, still rimed with natal blood; over the soft and fragile plates of his skull.

'Feed in peace, little parasite,' I whispered to him. 'I will see no harm comes to you. I will keep you safe.'

The rats came closer.

'In this Jungle, the weak are fodder for the

strong,' they said. 'There is no escape from the greed of the ruthless. At least the death we give is swift.'

I ignored them.

'I will take you away from here,' I whispered into the baby's ear, clutching him more tightly to me. 'This Jungle is a vile and dangerous place – full of hatred and hunger. We will leave here, you and I. We will go somewhere where the world is less mad. Where life is less twisted.'

'The only escape from the Jungle is death,' the rats said.

Their words filled me with the grave's chill. For I feared, deep inside, that they were right.

Sixteen

We left the Jondolo the next day, the child and I. I was weak still from the labour, and my torn vulva caused me considerable pain. But an urgency impelled me, anxiety for the child. I wanted him out of the stink of that place, away from the clamour of rats and corpses. The longer we stayed, the better the shadows would know him. I was afraid they would put their curse on him, that they would mark him for their own as they had marked me before him.

Yet it was not an easy thing to venture out of that lair – however noisome – and face the world again. For nine long months, I had skulked in hiding, setting foot outside only in the security of darkness, my only human contact, with the woman who nursed me. The daylit world seemed far too bright for me now. I felt too vivid in it, exposed to all eyes. My eyes, so long accustomed to the shack's gloom, watered in the morning sunlight as if with an over-abundance of tears.

I kept the baby clutched to me tightly, swaddled under my clothes, well-hidden. Invisibility, I knew, was his best defence. I did not want the Jungle's rapacious thoughts upon this morsel.

It seemed an interminable journey to Zach's hut. Progress was very slow. My weakness shocked me. It was not only the birth that had taken such toll of my strength, but the long preceding months of illness and injury, inactivity and little food. For the first time, I realized my own emaciation. My body was skeletal, my wasted limbs were the limbs of the child, Sorrow. I regretted my gaunt ugliness for Zach's sake. For I knew it would shock and distress him.

My mind dwelt with both eagerness and apprehension on our reunion. I had not dared to admit to myself the possibility that I might not find him at the hut, that he might have moved on somewhere else; or found his death at jakkal hands. A queer dissociation blanked my memory. The nine long months that stood between us seemed vague as a dream to me. I felt as if I was stepping back into a present that had not changed, from a sojourn in some other-dimension world, whose time-flow did not impact at all on this one. The prospect of seeing him again caused a wild mix of emotions to beat inside me. Longing was chief among them. But there was dread there too.

I was very fearful of the judgement of his eyes. For I was not the Marinda of nine months ago; no longer the frank and passionate child who had stood proclaiming her love for him beside the burning school. My nightmare had transfigured me. My breasts were scarred, my loins and womb invaded. My soul was the timid soul of a battered creature shrinking from each boot – lest it deliver further blows. And there was the child too, to explain. What words I would find for that, what Zach's reaction would be to them, I couldn't guess.

Yet all these worries were proved wasted in the end. For I did not find Zach at the hut. The air of desertion that hung over it spoke of a long abandonment. Scavengers had stripped it of everything movable; stove, curtains, mats – even our borehole tank was gone. The old blood marks still stained the door in their awfulness, filling me with shudders I couldn't control. I was glad to turn my back on it and make my slow, painful way down to the school. For that was the only place I could think of to ask for news of Zach. It was all rebuilt now, a solid, brickfaced phoenix risen from the ashes of its former self. I felt very alien standing in its unfamiliar shadow. It was impossible to believe that I had ever belonged here, that my face had worn the innocence and confidence of these faces around me. I saw none there that I recognized. And I was recognized by none. There was a new headmaster. When I enquired of him about Zach, he didn't know who I was talking about. The teachers were scarcely more helpful. It was months since any of them had seen him. No-one could say whether he was still alive or dead. Mostly, they had been too busy with their own troubles, with the rebuilding of the school to give him much thought. A few recalled that he had come by once or twice soon after the night of the fire, searching for me. What had become of him since then, they couldn't say.

Deeply dispirited, I trudged back to the hut. Its emptiness moaned like a dirge inside me. I couldn't bring myself to enter it, knowing the wounding ghosts that waited there. I stood hugging the baby to me, listening to the veld wind wail its bleak song in my ears;

'Lost – Lost – You have lost him forever! Forever.'

'No!' I told the baby. 'He isn't dead! I feel it – I know it! We'll find him, you and I. We'll search the world if we have to. But we will find him.'

I kissed his fuzzy infant head and sat down in the shade of the doorway to bare my breast for him. His greedy suckling reminded me of my own hunger. There was nothing for me to eat. My head swam with dizzy weakness. My body was full of trembling pain. I had no idea what to do next, where to go, how we were to survive. Our plight seemed very desperate to me. But for the baby's sake, I knew I could not give up. I watched his thirsty mouth contentedly drawing nourishment from my breast. And with every tiny tug, I felt my will grow stronger. Whatever happened, I was resolved that I would not take him back to the Jondolo. I knew too well what waited for him there. I would not have him grow up slave to shadows, his beauty warped by Kwashiorkor, his tender soul brutalized by Jungle cruelties. Somehow, we would find our escape from this nightmare. Nothing that awaited us in the world could be worse than what we left.

I stayed for the rest of the day at the hut, resting in its shelter, gathering my strength for the battles ahead. Dusk came. Then night. The wind grew cooler, blowing harder. But I bore with my shivers, loath to brave the hut's interior – even my small room; for I knew the memories I would meet with there. I lay with the baby's smallness cradled against me, watching the rush of clouds across the sky. Above them, stars blazed in their autumn constellations. I had forgotten their beauty, how the sky's wide freedom pleased me. I saw the Crux, lying like a bright diamond in the southern zenith. I saw Orion the great hunter, striding through his dark fields with his two dogs beside him. I watched whole galaxies spinning by.

'Take us with you!' I silently begged the stars. 'Save us from the rot and evil of this terrible Jungle. Take us anywhere.' And they answered me, saying; 'Follow us, follow us.'

When I slept, I dreamed of Zach. It was a very vivid dream. I was searching for him with the baby in my arms, through the rubble of the burned-down school. Only this rubble was endless, like the ruins of a city, a bomb-blasted world. A constant rain of ashes and charrings fell on my face, like the crisped bodies of locusts. I was trying in vain to keep the baby shielded from their black assault. I looked up out of my despair, and Zach was standing there, watching me, his face unsmiling, his head all tangled in stars.

'Zach!' I said. 'Zach – help us, show us the way out of this death-pit. Don't abandon us here!' And he answered me as the stars had, saying, 'Follow me, follow me.'

'Where?' I cried despairingly. 'I don't know where to find you! Tell me where you've gone!'

But the sky swept him up before he could answer. And he was borne away with the stars on the wind of the night.

Seventeen

I named the baby Isak – meaning, 'One who almost became the scapegoat,' after his namesake in the Bible. In unguarded moments, I would sometimes called him Zak – and the name would jolt through me like a shock of pain. He had Zach's unusual yellow eyes too – an unnerving co-incidence. Sometimes, those eyes seemed to me far too wise for such an infant face. As if the thoughts that moved behind them belonged to a far more sagacious soul.

He was a good baby from the start, crying seldom, stoic in the face of discomfort. With every day that passed, I loved him more. It was he who gave me the courage and tenacity to keep surviving through the hard days that followed our escape from the Jungle. And there were many hard days, particularly in the first months. Terrible though the Jungle was, at least I knew the shape of its evils. Familiarity made it seem like home. The world outside was huge and bewildering by comparison; utterly indifferent to us and our pathetic troubles. Everywhere, we were greeted with the suspicion reserved for strangers. What help we received was grudgingly given. We blew rootless from place to place, connected to nothing, wanted nowhere. It seemed to me that we were less free than before. The Jungle's long shadow bobbed at our shoulder, mocking us with its spectres of starvation and doom. In dreams, I saw it reaching out for us, sneering in the voice of the rats; 'Death is the only escape from the Jungle. The only escape.'

We survived, in those initial days, mainly by begging. Isak was far better at this game than I was. He knew, even at that tender age, how to melt hearts. His smile would beam out at the crucial moment, his babyish gurgles softening stern features into reluctant acquiescence, making hands reach more willingly into their pockets. Without him, I would have encountered much more often the brusqueness of the world's hard face.

Slowly though, surviving became easier. I became better-versed in the arts of itinerant living. I learnt to be less timid in my approaches to strangers, to present myself with confidence on their mercy. For confidence inspires confidence, whereas supplication draws only contempt. I discovered in myself too, a healing gift, like my mother's. I could lay my hands upon a swollen abdomen and draw the pain out. I could locate the cause of fever in a sick child, and heal with touch alone. This skill proved a very useful one to us. It bought us food and shelter, the lasting gratitude of its recipients. For where we went, there were often no doctors, and the nearest clinic was miles away. Now, far from being unwelcome, we were frequently pressed to stay. But restlessness drove me

111

onwards. The distance beckoned irresistibly. For somewhere in the distance, Zach was. I believed this with unshakeable certainty. My yearning for him pulsed like a deep-seated current, propelling me on through the world in an unceasing search; my course always southwards, where the Cross pointed. For south was where instinct impelled me. South was where the sea was, the mystical place of marvels, with which Zach's stories had so impressed my child's mind.

In every place we passed through, I asked for news of him.

But always, I was disappointed. It filled me with despair to realize how big the world was, how invisible one man could be among its multitudes. The one factor that gave me hope was Zach's distinctive colouring. There were not many brown men with his yellow hair and eyes. Those who did encounter him, would remember.

The months flowed by, fusing almost unnoticed into each other. Isak's first birthday came and went. And suddenly, he was not a helpless infant anymore, but a lively toddler. He was still small in size, but robust with it – straight and healthy, full of chuckles and endearing naughtiness. His unblemished growth filled me with the deepest joy and gratitude. There was nothing of the slave in his spirit. A feisty confidence shone from his yellow eyes. It pleased me to see how he thrived on this life of wandering freedom. It made all the hardships of our early days seem worthwhile. I watched over his well-being like a ferocious she-hawk, alert to every hint of hazard. For his sake, we kept as much as possible to country routes, avoiding the larger settlements and cities. For they smelled too strongly of shadow for my liking, too full of decomposing souls.

Isak loved the country. He had a deep empathy towards all natural things. He could sit content and quiet for hours under some spreading tree, watching the dance of its leaves in the wind, talking his infant talk to the parade of insect life on its bark. The flight of birds held the same fascination for him as it once had for me. Butterflies caused beaming smiles to break out. Remembering my own deprived upbringing in the denuded Jungle wasteland, it gave me infinite pleasure to see his pleasure in these things.

One day, after a long trek through sparsely settled farmland, we came to a small settlement, set amid sugar cane hills. I asked the usual questions there about Zach, steeling myself for the usual disappointing replies. But this time, my enquiries brought response.

'The fiddler, do you mean?' a woman said.

My heart flew into my throat.

'Yes!' I said. 'You have seen him here then?'

'He was here,' she nodded. 'A few weeks back. Maybe more. I remember him well. His fiddling could wring tears from stars. The shebeen* owners were always glad to have him on their premises. For his melancholy playing boosted their drink sales like nothing else!'

'Do you know where he went when he left here?' I asked her.

* Shebeen = place where alcoholic drinks are sold illegally

She shook her head. 'He may have mentioned something. I can't recall now.'

'Try!' I beseeched her.

She saw on my face why the information was so important to me. 'I really can't recall,' she said regretfully. 'But my cousin might know. The fiddler lodged with him a night or two. He might have mentioned it to him.'

Her cousin wasn't at home, however. And his wife was not inclined to be helpful. It wasn't hard to guess what lay behind her surly attitude. I saw the jealous suspicion of her gaze as it probed over Isak.

'What strange eyes he has, your child,' she said to me insinuatingly. 'Yellow is a very uncommon colour for eyes. The fiddler had eyes that colour too. I remember remarking on them.'

Just then her husband returned. He was far more friendly and forthcoming than his wife had been.

'The fiddler – yes – he stayed here with us a few nights. Zach, I think he said his name was. Strange, silent fellow,' he said pensively.

It hurt me to hear what my bright Shadowslayer had become.

'He did not like to talk too much about himself,' the man mused on. 'There was some deep sadness weighing on him. He only spoke of it through his fiddling. By the earth, but he could twist your heart with that fiddling of his!'

'Did he say where he was going to from here?' I asked the man.

He shook his head. 'Not to me. He didn't really know himself, I think. He was just drifting where the wind took him. Strange man, as I have said. But I liked him.'

'I liked him also,' piped up the man's small daughter. 'He told me stories. About a girl who could talk to cockroaches. He wore a funny necklace that she gave him. He said it saved his life once. But I didn't like that story. Its ending was too sad.'

Tears burst under my eyelids, swamping my vision, blinding me for a second.

'Did he tell you anything else? Any other stories?' I asked the little one, crouching down to look into her small, sweet face.

'There was one about a Sea,' she nodded shyly. 'It was all shining and'...' she struggled to remember. '. . . all the beauty in the world lived there and . . . He said he was going there too. To listen to the waves talk.'

'He must have meant Hele Hele. The Place Of Breezes' smiled her father.

I looked at him, hardly able to breathe for the hope that was choking my throat.

'There is such a place?' I asked him, my voice faint as a whisper.

'Yes,' he assured me. 'I have been there myself. It is a very beautiful spot, not too far away from here. Where the river runs into the sea.'

A trembling urgency overcame me. My feet wanted to fly there instantly.

'How can I get there? Can you tell me the way?' I asked the man.

'Better than that. I can find you a lift there. I know of trucks that regularly go in that direction.

One of them would be willing to take you, I'm sure.' He winked at me with kindly sympathy. 'For I can see that you are in a hurry for this reunion!'

'It has been a long parting,' was all I told him.

That night, we slept, Isak and I, in our benefactor's house, camping down on the narrow mattress in his little daughter's room, where before us, Zach had camped. Sleep was very far from me that night. I lay awake well into the small hours, breathing the room's air that Zach had breathed, imagining I felt still the imprint of his body on the mattress beneath me. When at last I did sleep, my dreams were full of the violin's voice. I heard its dark·pain calling to me across black distances, urgent and compelling. But no matter how I searched, I could not track the sound to its source.

The next morning, true to his word, our host found us a passage on a truck bound for the coast, and before the sun rose, we were on our way once more. I sat perched like queen of the cabbages, on a truckbed full of the vegetables, Isak resting contentedly on my lap. Green sugarcane hills swam by, draped in the mist of the morning, and the blue of the sky seemed to promise only good things. The salt smell of the breeze made my stomach churn with fearful expectation. I listened to the rumble of the tyres on the rough road, thundering out the syllables of Zach's name – and felt the racing rhythm of my heart, keeping pace with the speeding wheels.

Eighteen

Hele Hele is a place of music – and of meetings. The river joins the sea here, the sea joins the sky. And all the world seems fluid and shining and infinite. Blue is the colour of things here; sky blue, sea blue, dazzling your eyes with its unfiltered beauty. White gulls drift, yelping on the wind-tides. The great sea thunders and sighs like a dreaming dragon, tossing its restless coils in the grip of the sun's silver nets. The air is full of the chiming of wind and the sighing of water. It is all exactly as Zach's stories described it to me. I stood with Isak pressed against my legs, tears in my eyes, staring at the spectacle in wonderment and pain. Isak broke free from my hold and ran, laughing, to challenge the rush and roar of the waves. Their flung spray bathed my face like salty sorrow. The deep note of longing that boomed from the sea's throat found its echo in my own.

Further down the beach, I saw a band of fishermen, wading through the foamy shallows, uncovering sea lice with their toes. I asked them about Zach. They all knew of the yellow-haired fiddler. A silent, sad man, they said, who could melt the heart of rocks with his stirring playing. He had been here for some weeks. But whether he was here still, or had since moved on, they couldn't be certain. He kept so much to himself, coming and going according to his own rhythms. They pointed out to me the direction of his hut and said I should ask there.

I trudged across the white expanse of sand, Isak dancing at my side, crowing to himself as he tumbled and raced on the sand's yielding surface. But my legs were leaden, my spirits very low. The possibility that we might have come here too late, that Zach might already have moved on, made me desolate. The beauty of this Place Of Breezes seemed suddenly to lose all its shine, its promise wounding like betrayal.

We rounded a curve of the dunes, followed a sandy path through low, thick-leaved dune scrub, towards a small gathering of fishermen's huts ahead. Away from the friendly cluster, a single dwelling stood brooding on its own, its face turned to the sea. I knew without being told that that one was Zach's. Full of inward trembling, I made towards it, Isak's hand tightly gripped in mine. There was no movement near it, no sign of life or habitation, inside or out. I stopped, too nervous to go on, steeling myself for the inevitable disappointment. Isak gazed up at me solemnly, sensing my distress. Kneeling, I gathered him to me. And as I did so, something caught my eye. Against the pale stem of a banana tree, a small, slender-shaped object rested, its gleaming brown surface catching the sunlight, leaf-shadow dancing on its strings. I stared at it, all breath frozen, the sight of it filling my vision till I could see nothing else. Movement shuddered in the gloom of the doorway. A figure came out. A tall, thin man, dressed in the casual garb of a fisherman, with a fisherman's knapsack in his hand. He stood staring vaguely out at nothing, as if searching the horizon for some signal to give purpose to his next move. He was a stranger to me, this man. I did not recognize his thinness. Or the way he stood so tired and defeated, his shoulders stooping as though he carried the world's weight on them. But the yellow hair was Zach's hair. There was no mistaking that.

Tears ran from my eyes at the sight of that beloved vividness. I let go of Isak's hand and walked forward blindly.

'Zach,' I said, 'Zach.'

He looked at me without interest, without recognition, sunlight dazzling his eyes. He shielded his face with his hand and looked again. I saw the shock of recognition come into his eyes. He stared at me as one stares at a ghost, refusing to believe. His lips moved. They said – 'Marinda!'

But no sound came out.

'It's me. It is me,' I told him, my voice shaking like wind crossing an abyss. We were only ten paces apart now. But it felt as though a universe of time-space lay between us. Our separate hells had made us strangers to each other.

'I thought I'd lost you forever,' Zach said. 'I thought you were dead. You just disappeared! I thought . . .' He looked behind me suddenly. And he saw the child there. All joy drained from his face.

'Yours?' he asked. His voice was very flat.

'Yes,' I answered. There was no more that I could say, then.

He was silent for a time, looking at me.

'Well, I am glad to see you safe at any rate,' he said, guarding his eyes from me. 'I thought, as I said, that you were dead. I searched for you everywhere. I tried everything to find out what had happened to you. Then I gave up hope.'

'I never gave up hope of finding you,' I said.

His head jerked in surprise. His eyes went to the child again.

And I could read the thoughts that moved behind them.

'It's not what you think, Zach,' I told him.

'What is it then?' he challenged.

I struggled to find the words to tell him. 'Yes, the child is mine. And I love him now more than my life. But he was not the product of love, I assure you. I was not a willing partner in his conception. He was . . . forced into me with the worst brutality.' I could not help my shudders as I said it. 'I have the scars to prove it. It was . . . I was . . .'

But I couldn't go on. Neither could I bring myself to look into Zach's face; I was too afraid of finding condemnation there.

'Oh Marinda!' he said. There was shock in his voice, grief and horror. 'I had no idea! I didn't know! Oh forgive me!'

He put a hand towards me, took it back again, as though fearful I might flinch from his touch.

'When did this happen?' he asked me hoarsely. 'How?'

'It doesn't matter now,' I said, struggling to swallow the bitter taste of the memory.

'But why didn't you come to me? Why did you hide yourself away like that? Didn't you know I would have helped you through this thing? There was no need for you to bear it alone!'

'I couldn't come to you,' I said in a low voice. 'I couldn't let you see what had been done to me. I felt too much loathing for myself. Don't ask me more,' I begged. 'Not now.'

The child toddled forward to clutch my leg, staring up at the tall man with curious eyes. The sight of Zach's bright hair seemed to catch his fancy. A sudden smile beamed out of him, lighting his chubby features with endearing sunniness.

'He has your smile, this little one,' Zach said, reaching down his hand to fondle the child's small head.

'And your eyes, Zach.'

I saw the jolt my words gave him. He took his hand back quickly, pain searing his face.

'He has your spirit in him too,' I continued softly. 'Don't ask me to explain it. He is the child that should have been conceived between us that night at the school.'

Zach looked at me in silence, his thoughts impossible to read.

'You thought me too young for love then, remember?' I said, a trifle bitterly. 'Too young for love. But not for rape.' I saw him flinch at the words. His hand reached out to my mouth – to

121

silence it or caress it was not certain. He rubbed his thumb over my lips. Then placed his own lips there. The sweetness of the kiss drowned us both. He lifted his head away to look at me. And I saw, flickering in his eyes, the old irrepressible Shadow-slayer's light.

'The first time that I saw you,' he said, 'you were hardly much taller than the child here. You had red Kwashiorkor hair. And your face was so thin and hungry that it cut my heart like a knife. I asked you what you were doing there. And you said . . .'

' . . . that I was talking to the cockroaches. And you gave me my name, Marinda.' I pressed myself, trembling against him. 'When you name something, it belongs to you forever,' I whispered.

He hooked his arm around my head and drew me to him with a fierceness that was almost like violence. We stood leaning together like two storm-battered trees, drawing strength from each other's bodies.

'Never leave me again!' Zach whispered fervently against my mouth. 'My heart can't bear it!'

'Never! Never!' I answered, shaking against him like a reed in wild water.

We hugged each other like drowning people, the child sandwiched, forgotten, between us. I heard his deep-throated chuckles as he squirmed amid the forest of our legs.

Zach reached down to heft him up into our embrace, grinning as the chubby fists reached instantly to clutch at his alluring bright hair.

'What's his name?' he asked me, rubbing his gaunt cheek against the silky infant one.

I told him.

'It's a good name,' he nodded. 'There's strength in it. And luck too.'

He passed his hand lightly over the child's head and whispered into his ear; 'Isak. Isak.'

Isak's head turned to regard him solemnly. And the look that passed between those yellow-eyed stares – so alike, so beloved, brought a gush of tears to my eyes.

We live, these days, a simple life together, Zach, Isak and I. And yes, I dare to say that we are happy. We wander the world like gypsies still, wherever the wind directs us. For the itinerant habit, once acquired, is not an easy one to break. Rooted in each other, we feel no need to put down roots. Though sometimes . . sometimes, I suspect there is a different reason for our restlessness.

We seldom speak of the Jungle. But it preys on both our minds, I think. Although we have escaped its clutches, we cannot forget the many suffering souls still left behind there, living their trapped lives under the tyranny of evil. I think that we will never go back, however. For we have been tested to the limits of our endurance. We have learnt the hard lessons of shadows – that even a Shadow-slayer's courage sometimes is no match for the ruthlessness of evil.

Isak now; he is a different case. Already, even at his young age, I see in him the makings of a Shadow-slayer. He has all Zach's tenderness towards suffering and defenceless things. But something else besides; a hint of steel. When his protective ire is roused, he can be as ruthless as any predator. Young as he is, this quality is apparent to me. Whether this has to do with the circumstances of his conception, I can only guess at. I remember what my good friends the cockroaches used to tell me; the poison of snakes makes the best anti-venom.

I look across the future sometimes. And I see my son there, striding tall and bright and invincible through the shadows of this world. I think – I know – that the Jungle has not seen the last of him. When he returns there, it will be with the avenging might of angels on his side. And the jakkals shall have cause to rue his sting!